Praise for *The Water Is Wide*

"Mima's journey across the water is a journey of faith. Every girl can relate to it because ultimately every girl has to know the truth for herself. I adore this book!"

—Laurel Christensen, author of *He Loves Us, and We Love Him: You've Memorized It, Now Live It* (coming October 2010)

"*The Water Is Wide* is *our* story, for either we have ancestors who left familiar surroundings because of their faith in the restored gospel or we will be that person for those who follow us. This is a book I couldn't put down, and I wholeheartedly recommend it!"

—Jack Weyland, author of *Charly* and *It All Started with Autumn Jones*

"*The Water Is Wide* is like powerfully written music. The ebb and flow of emotion, the beautiful detail, and the dynamics of Mima's fascinating story all combined in a melody that inspired and moved me."

—Jenny Phillips author of *The Parable of the Go*

D0348850

THE MIMA · *Book One* · JOURNALS

The Water
Is Wide

THE MIMA · *Book One* · JOURNALS

The Water Is Wide

MARIANNE MONSON

DESERET
BOOK

SALT LAKE CITY, UTAH

JEMIMA RUSHBY HOUGH MIDGLEY

MY GREAT-GREAT-GREAT-GRANDMOTHER

Library of Congress Cataloging-in-Publication Data
Monson, Marianne, 1975–
   The water is wide / Marianne Monson.
      p. cm. — (The Mima journals ; bk. 1)
   Summary: When Mima's mother meets a pair of Mormon missionaries in the small English town of Wooden Box in 1845, Mima prays that the townspeople won't treat them any differently. But when her mother chooses to be baptized, Mima's worst fears are realized. Even her best friend refuses to stand by her. So when her mother decides to leave for America, Mima is faced with some hard decisions.
   ISBN 978-1-60641-841-3 (paperbound)
   1. Mormon converts—England—History—19th century—Fiction. 2. Mormon pioneers—Fiction. I. Title. II. Series: Monson, Marianne, 1975–
Mima journals ; bk. 1.
   PS3613.O539W38 2010
   813'.6—dc22   2010019369

Printed in the United States of America
Publishers Printing, Salt Lake City, UT

10 9 8 7 6 5 4 3 2 1

ACKNOWLEDGMENTS

I owe a great debt of gratitude to those who helped with the research and writing of this book. Scholars at Brigham Young University who graciously assisted with the historical research include Professors Brent L. Top, Susan Easton Black, and William G. Hartley. Lachlan Mackay at Community of Christ provided invaluable knowledge of the early Church in Nauvoo. Joan Neff provided information about vocal performance and technique. The Bishop of Gloucester answered many questions about the Church of England, and the Trinity Episcopal Cathedral in Portland welcomed me as a visitor. The Midgley family in Yorkshire, England, introduced me to the region and took me to visit parish churches and graves. Karen and Audrey Hough, in London, distant relatives and descendants of Jemima, provided me with extensive information about the area. Clyde Dissington at the Magic Attic was an invaluable resource for all things related to family history, and I am quite sure that the missionaries at

ACKNOWLEDGMENTS

the Church History Library of The Church of Jesus Christ of Latter-day Saints in Salt Lake City are modern-day angels.

I am thankful to family and friends for reading early versions of the manuscript, particularly Danielle and Marilynn Monson. I owe an enormous debt to Heidi Taylor at Deseret Book Company for loving Mima from the beginning and renewing my enthusiasm for the project. Also to my dedicated professors at Vermont College, without whom this book would never have been written: Kathi Appelt, Marion Dane Bauer, Liza Ketchum, and Laura Kvasnosky. Finally I thank my grandmothers for raising me on pioneer stories, and my children, Nathan and Aria, who listen to my stories today.

Part One

WOODEN BOX, LEICESTERSHIRE, ENGLAND

JANUARY 1845

CHAPTER ONE

*O*ur song filled up the cold, empty spaces of St. Peter's parish church. The hymn bounced along the grand stone arches, mellowed with the colors of the stained glass, and settled into the worn, wooden pews.

I loved the sound. It was a sound I had heard my whole life. As a baby, I'd been brought by Mother and Father to this parish church for services: a chubby infant in white muslin ruffles, sitting between them in our own wooden pew. The sound of the service must have filled up my baby ears because when Mother tells the story she says, "Mima, you would open your mouth and sing with the choir on one very loud, very flat note." Even then I knew I wanted to sing.

From my place in the choir stalls, I glanced at my family's empty pew. Father was in his grave. Mother was at home. I refused to think of why.

Old Mrs. Robinson sat in the pew behind, her eyes as sharp as a hawk. She nodded at me and a faint smile crossed her lips. My cheeks flaring red, I turned away. Could those hawk eyes have read my secret?

"Glory be to the Father and the Son," we sang. My voice melted into the other voices of the choir. The sound was whole and good.

The cold stone angles of the church echoed the song, drawing out each note. The sound was otherworldly, mystical, magical, unfathomable—like God, I thought.

Rector Buckley recited a psalm. "O let me be delivered from them that hate me, and out of the deep waters. Let not the water-flood drown me, neither let the deep swallow me up."

I shivered in spite of my warm serge dress. The words made the church even darker and colder. Rector Buckley's Voice (I always thought of it with a Capital Letter) was deep and gravelly. It was his Voice, more than his words, that made me think of such majestic places as heaven and hell. His Voice was like a Bach fugue, deep and sonorous. He had been rector at St. Peter's since before I was born. Since before Mother came to Wooden Box to marry Father. Perhaps he had been rector since the psalms were first recorded. I would not have been surprised.

"For God will save Zion, and build the cities of Judah that men may dwell there," he chanted.

Where is Zion? I wondered. Canterbury? Jerusalem? I pictured a white city across a stormy sea.

The congregation had been lulled into a trance by Rector Buckley. There were a handful of members. Only the stalwart and faithful of Hartshorne walked through the snow to Vespers. The Midgleys and their three boys. The boys were usually squirrelly, but they could not wriggle when the Voice was rumbling. Miss Elizabeth Parker, an old maid, nodded her head in time with the service. Mrs. Robinson looked pious. The Eldredges and the Parsons. They all could remember me as that baby who wanted to sing. What would they say if they knew my secret?

A flash of black leather was followed by a sharp pain in my toe. I looked at Charlotte. Her eyebrows were knotted together in alarm. I thanked her with a sheepish glance and then opened my mouth, without time to think of pitch. My voice wavered for a moment until it settled on the true note. High C. *Glory be to the Father . . .* The other voices joined my own.

> *And to the Son:*
> *and to the Holy Ghost;*
> *as it was in the beginning,*
> *is now, and ever shall be:*
> *worlds without end. Amen.*

My breath hung in the frosty air, and the sound slipped into the shadows of the church. Vespers was over. Charlotte gave my hand a consoling squeeze as the Burtons, Miss Parker, Mrs. Robinson, the Eldredges, and the Parsons slipped from the pews and out the door. Their feet shuffled and scraped, but in the tradition of Evensong, they did not speak.

Charlotte tied her bonnet and looked at me with a dimpled smile. She was teasing me without words. Charlotte could tease and look angelic at the same time, one of the benefits of having golden curls and round, pink lips. I grinned and wrapped my cloak about me.

Rector Buckley nodded at us, and we were released into the night.

Charlotte and I walked a few yards from the church before she dared to whisper. The other choir girls looked after us, scandalized, but Charlotte did not care. "I thought you were never going to sing," she said. "In another moment Rector Buckley was going to start the song for you."

"I would love to have heard that," I said. "His Voice is charming for prayer, but it doesn't sound much like a choir girl's."

Charlotte covered her mouth to hold back a giggle.

"He must despise me." I glanced furtively back at the church to make sure Rector Buckley was not in earshot and then smiled at my friend.

"Of course not," she replied. "He may not like your daydreams, but only you could manage to begin on the correct note, even when you're not paying the least bit attention. Whatever were you thinking of, Mima?"

A black pain tore at my heart. I longed to tell her. I had never kept a secret from her before. Did I dare?

"Nothing," I replied at last. "I must be tired."

"Good-night, Mima." She kissed my cheek, and I smelled lavender. Then she pulled her cloak tight and became yet another shadow hurrying into the village of Hartshorne. I was alone with my shame.

CHAPTER TWO

I left Hartshorne and reached the High Street. The road rose gradually up to the bridge, a precipice between the two villages. Hartshorne lay behind me, and Wooden Box lay ahead, its pottery factories shaped like mammoth beehives, brooding in the dark. The stone arches, draped windows, and puffing chimneys were wrapped in a blanket of November frost and silence.

The melodies of Evensong played on in my head, but I could not sing or even hum. The world was too silent, with only the sweep of my skirts brushing over the snow to break the stillness.

The distant tower of St. Margaret's, where Father lies, the toll booth, the quaint shops along the High Street, and the lane that winds to Providence House were all smudged over with shadows, like a picture with an ink blot too dark to remove. My black boots crunched on the crisp rime of frost, and my breath, heavy with steam, hung in the air. It seemed wrong to be out on a night such as this when the moon and the frost bade me go inside.

Yet I did not wish to be inside. My steps slowed as I neared the turn to Providence House. Dear Providence House. The only home I had ever known, with its grand parlor and quaint gables and oddly slanting roof line. A place that makes me think of spring, when the honeysuckle and cabbage roses climbed over the windows and wrapped the air of the house in a thick and dreamy smell.

But that night I did not want to enter the house I loved. I longed to keep walking so I would not have to hear the words I feared my mother would say. Words that could change our lives—so settled and centered here—forever. I thought briefly of running away with gypsies. I considered asking Charlotte's parents to adopt me.

"Be practical," I envisioned Mother saying. "Few things are ever as awful as you imagine them to be."

I sighed and opened the door.

CHAPTER THREE

The house was dark except for a light burning from the only room at Providence House I did not enjoy. It was Mother's favorite room: her sewing room and shop. Her voice floated toward me drawing me to the light. "Mima, is that you?"

"Yes, Mother," I called as I shut the door. Martha, our maid, greeted me, brushing the snow from my cloak as she hung it up, before she returned to the kitchen. I wished I could join her there.

The sewing shop had held a certain fascination when I was a child. The shelves, lined neatly with packages, were labeled with such intriguing names as Corset Lining, Poplar Muslin, Whalebone Stays, Silver Thimbles, and Silk Embroidery Thread.

But I soon realized that time in the shop meant lengths of linen scrim for samplers, samplers that required me to sit still in a chair and use a steel needle to count tiny threads. One, two, three, four; cross-stitch, down two, three, four; tent stitch, over two, three, four; stem stitch; and back again. After several months I had as a reward for my efforts a piece of cloth with words embroidered across it: "Jemima Rushby Hough is my name. Lord guide my life that I may do Thy will and fill my hands with such convenient skill as will conduce to virtue void of shame and will lend glory to Thy name." When I remembered all the ill-feelings that had been worked into that sampler, it seemed rather unlikely that the dutiful message had had the desired result.

As I entered the room, Mother looked up from her seat at the embroidery frame. A fire burned in the fireplace, and Mother had lit a candle at either end of the frame. She was embroidering a cloak for Mrs. Merrick, promised in two day's time.

She was eager to see me—*too* eager. I longed to run back down the stairs. But Mother beckoned to me. "Bring the new thread from the spinning wheel, Mima."

"Very well," I said.

Mother adored learning the latest fashions of the needle. She spent long hours devising her own patterns for the tambour lace she made on sheer mull. If she wasn't working on a project for a customer, she was embroidering a new case for a prayer book or doing her beloved Berlin work in brilliant worsteds. Every chair at Providence House had a Berlin pillow or seat, every table had a mat. She carried sewing necessities with her everywhere, clasped around her waist in a small silver chatelaine, a gift from my father shortly before he died.

I removed my bonnet and cloak and laid them on the settee. "It's bitter cold tonight," I said. "Precious few came to Evensong." I glanced at her head, bent piously over her work.

Was it possible she was really my mother? We were nothing alike. She was a short, sturdy woman. I was tall like my father. "My hair used to be chestnut brown, just like yours," she often said. But I could not recall her hair any color but charcoal gray, parted down the middle and pulled into a twist. She was as old as Charlotte's grandmother. Her skin was still remarkably smooth and supple, though, her nose straight and firm, her mouth a thin line. Her eyes were blue and clear. She was everything a good seamstress must be: steady, patient, and practical. Not at all like me.

I pulled the soft fibers from the wheel and sat beside her, studying the pattern she had begun along the border of the cloak. Separating a single filament, I chose a needle from the emery, threaded it, and knotted the end until it looked much like my stomach felt. I trimmed the thread and sighed again. As much as I disliked the labor, I could have done it in my sleep. The needle pierced deep into the cloth.

"You are using a stem stitch?" I asked.

Mother nodded and leaned close to me, as if for reassurance. I knew her mind was not on the stitching. "I liked the meeting, Mima," she said, speaking the words I did not want to hear. "I liked it very much."

I closed my eyes against the sound of her voice, willing her to stop. "Yes, Mother," I murmured. I jabbed with the needle, piercing the cloth.

"I would like to join the Mormon congregation, daughter." Her fingers moved faster now, sewing steadily. "I feel God's presence at the meetings."

"Just as at St. Peter's," I said, wishing my voice did not shake.

"There is a difference." Mother sewed at a constant pace. She did not miss a stitch. I wondered how she could sew such careful, small stitches.

Mother always said my emotions showed in my stitches, and she was right. I looked at the uneven line I had just finished and knew I would be picking it out come morning.

"I know it is the truth," she continued. "God has called a new prophet. He is speaking to the earth once again." Her voice burned with certainty.

"You *know* this? How could you claim to know this?" I jabbed again with my needle, like a lance to my foe.

"I simply know it, daughter. The Holy Spirit testifies of truth, and I have felt it." Her stitches were fast overtaking mine. Soon she would tie the end of her thread to the beginning of my own. They would run together. Hers, swift and sure; mine, crude and lopsided.

"Mormons go to America. Is the Mormon truth enough to leave Providence House? Will you go too?" I held my breath, awaiting her response.

"No. Of course not, Mima. I would not leave you." Her voice was steady and slow. My breath escaped in a rush.

"Mormons don't all go to America," she continued. "I will follow the Mormon ways here."

With this assurance, anger suddenly swelled inside until I thought my chest might burst. "Then join them," I said. "Join the dissenters, if you must." The venom on my tongue was plain. My mind spun. Would they allow the daughter of a dissenter to lead the choir? Would Miss Pritchard want a dissenter as a pupil? Would I be allowed to marry in St. Peter's, when and if anyone allowed their son to marry into such a family? I wondered if Mother had thought of any of this—the effect it would have on everything in my future. How long would it take for the town to find out? For Charlotte to find out?

"But, daughter, you must also know that the Mormon truth *is* enough. That if I had to give up everything, it would still be enough."

I was stunned, but she did not seem to notice.

"I believe you would like the Mormon meetings. They sing the most beautiful songs."

I dropped the needle as if it had stung me, then flung it from me as if it were a Mormon tract. She carefully placed her needle on the cloak and met my eyes at last. They were filled with sorrow.

"I will never sing a Mormon song," I said. My voice still shook, but this time it was with resolve instead of fear. "I will never attend a Mormon meeting. I will never be a Mormon. And if you choose to join them, you will regret it until your life ends."

As I ran from the room, Mother called after me, but I did not stop, and her cry chased me, demon-like, out the door.

CHAPTER FOUR

*F*or a week I agonized, hesitant in every conversation. When Mrs. Wight asked, "How is your mother?" I eyed her cautiously before answering.

When a friend said, "Will you be at church tonight?" I thought, *Surely she must know.*

But at other moments I told myself that perhaps no one would ever know. Perhaps Mother would go discreetly to her meetings and life could continue unchanged. Or perhaps people would find out, and they would care little. Perhaps Charlotte already knew and did not speak of it for kindness. I clutched at the hope like a hungry dog after a scrap.

But a week later, I was in the shop with Mother when Mrs.

Merrick arrived. Mother put down her work and went to greet her. "Good afternoon, Mrs. Merrick."

"Good afternoon," said Mrs. Merrick. I looked up from my stitching at the note of formality in her voice.

"Mrs. Hough, I have heard some news that I wish to know the truth of," said Mrs. Merrick. "I hope it is only idle rumor, but it has been said that you plan to join the Mormons."

The smile fell from Mother's face. "It is true," said Mother. "I am joining their congregation. But Mima and I plan to stay in the Box."

Mrs. Merrick's face grew hard. "I am very sorry to hear that it is true. I have always considered you to be a sensible woman. I'm sure you can understand that I will not do business with a dissenter. Good day." Her words were as crisp and cold as the snow outside. With a swirl of her cloak in the doorway, she was gone.

Shame and relief washed over me. Shame at our secret, and a strange relief that it had been acknowledged. At least now I would not have to speak about everything except my true thoughts. I dropped my sewing and crossed the room to press my fingers to the frigid window, watching Mrs. Merrick mount her carriage.

Mother sighed and returned to her Berlin work.

"How did she learn of it?" I asked.

"Ann Harrison saw me walking with the Mormon missionaries two days ago. No doubt she has spread the news."

"Mrs. Harrison?" I gasped. She was Father's daughter, born of his first wife. My half-sister would love to spread such news of us. How could Mother be so careless? "It will be all over town, then."

Mother nodded. A deep sense of dread settled at the bottom of my stomach.

Two days later Mrs. Swift and Miss Raney came to call for a similar purpose. Even Mrs. Hannah Buckley retrieved a length of black velvet she had given to Mother for a cloak. Mother had made her wedding gown and then her baby's christening gown. "I have decided to save it for another purpose," she said, avoiding Mother's eyes, though all of us knew she had not spoken the truth.

On Friday when Mother counted the earnings from the week, a furrow of worry creased her brow.

I watched her with innocent eyes. "Can you afford to be a Mormon?" I asked.

Mother ignored my rudeness and only sighed. "I scarcely know," she said.

CHAPTER FIVE

On Tuesday I walked to St. Peter's for choir rehearsal. My feet dragged of their own accord, and I arrived a few minutes late. When I entered the church, I heard whispers and giggles that immediately stopped when the door closed behind me.

"Hello, Mima," said Charlotte.

"We weren't sure you'd be coming," said Clara, a girl two years older than I. Her voice was smooth and even, but I felt the barb hidden within.

"I am not ill," I said, throwing her a meaningful glance.

She fell silent and turned away.

We sang several pieces, but when we paused, the seven other girls were suddenly busy with conversation, and I was left standing alone. I waited, hoping it was only an accident. I examined my gloves.

Then Kate Merrick did turn to me, but her eyes were cold. "How is your mother?" she asked.

"She is well," I said. My eyes dared her to continue.

"Do you know, Mima, at dinner last night my father said he would prefer we run off with the gypsies than with the Mormons? He said that with the gypsies we would be better cared for."

"So are you planning your trip, then?" I asked sweetly.

Kate's face flushed. "*Your* trip is more likely. Is your mother really going to America?"

The church was incredibly quiet. "No, of course not," I replied. "She's staying here."

"Mormons always leave," Kate said. "Whether they want to or not. How long will it be before she convinces you to join?" A few of the girls snickered.

"I am not joining," I said. I wished I could think of a scathing reply. But Kate was right. Mormons usually did leave. And suddenly I could understand why. Perhaps it became too hard to stay.

"Let her alone, Kate," said Charlotte. "You're none too eager to talk about your brother, after all."

It was Kate's turn to color, and I looked at Charlotte with relief. Kate's brother had moved to Liverpool when it became clear that the family's maid would soon have his child. But Charlotte did not walk toward me, as I thought she would. Her eyes rested on me for a moment before she turned away.

Finally, we returned to our practice. As we sang, it seemed that I no longer blended seamlessly with the others. My own voice seemed to stand apart from the others, separate somehow. Try as I might, I no longer fit in. The balance was ruined.

When rehearsal was finished, I wanted to run home. As I left the church, Charlotte called after me. *Finally,* I thought. But her embrace was not as warm as usual.

"Is it true?" she asked, and for once her blue eyes were serious.

I nodded. "Mother wants to join the Mormons. I cannot convince her to forget the nonsense. But she plans to stay here."

Charlotte looked unconvinced.

"Would you like to come home with me?" I asked. "You haven't been over in ages."

"Don't you know what they're saying?" she asked.

I shook my head.

"They say that Mormons delude their followers, using devilish mind-altering until they do whatever they are asked."

"That's ridiculous," I said.

"My mother doesn't think so," said Charlotte.

"You have never cared what people thought before," I said.

Charlotte shook her curls. "I'm sorry, Mima, but I think they are right to be careful." She pressed my hand and turned away.

As I watched her go, I tried to convince myself that this was real. Charlotte and I had seldom been apart since we were babies. Together we defied everyone and everything. Did she really believe Mother had been bewitched? As she darted back into the church, leaving me in the churchyard, I felt I had never before understood the meaning of the word *alone.*

CHAPTER SIX

*E*lder Russell removed his hat, clasped his hands together, and began to pray. His lips moved, but I refused to listen to his words. Instead I watched the December sun, pale and spiritless, striving to fall upon his bare head and then saw it retreat, exhausted with the effort. It seemed that snow had forever cooled the warmth of the sun on this ice-bound day. I wiggled my toes in their black boots and found I could feel them faintly. Elder Russell was still praying, and I stared at his bare head, without bothering to hide my hatred.

He finished the prayer and looked up, straight into my eyes. He held my gaze for a moment, as if he could read the pounding message of my heart. I looked away, ashamed. My eyes fell upon Mother, standing beside Elder Russell and blushing like a young bride. In the dull light, her hair was white, her clothes were white, the land and even the sky were white. It was unearthly.

If Mother felt the cold, she did not show it, and I marveled yet again at the change in her. Oftentimes I felt as though our roles had been reversed: that she was the daughter, rushing into this foolishness, and I was the mother, cursing her brash behavior. It was an eerie feeling, the feeling that you must keep your mother under control. And although I had told her I would never attend a Mormon meeting, there I was, watching as she was baptized.

I thought she might reconsider when I said, "You have already been baptized. In St. Margaret's. Why would you need baptizing again?"

"Because there was no authority the first time," she had said.

"Rector Buckley has no authority?" I was puzzled. "After taking vows and being approved by the Queen?"

"I wish to be baptized by one whose authority comes from God, daughter."

I did not ask how Elder Russell happened to have received this authority from God when Rector Buckley had not. I was sure she had a reason for it—she had a reason for everything now—but I did not care to know.

I had failed. This day was proof of that, this circle of fifteen or so Mormon men and women and children, too, all smiling and shaking hands, congratulating themselves on having convinced one more to follow, convinced through their devilish ways, perhaps. And now my mother, who could not swim, who barely dared wade ankle deep in water, was about to be plunged into Repton Brook in the middle of

December—and she was smiling. I remembered Charlotte's whispers about mind-altering.

I glared anew at Elder Russell's head, now covered. He was addressing the group, and I listened to his words in spite of myself. "And so baptism is a sacred promise," he said, "signifying to our Father in Heaven that we will walk here with the Savior, following his example of goodness. And when we promise to follow the Savior Jesus Christ, we promise to do our utmost to live the kind of life he lived—simple, humble, full of charity, and above all, willing to sacrifice everything to the greatness of this gospel he has entrusted to us."

My mind caught hold of his words: "willing to sacrifice everything." Everything. Money, Providence House, friends, and family. Mother had sacrificed plenty of money. In addition to the loss of customers, Rector Buckley reminded her that dissenters were responsible for paying the church tax, something I had never thought about because I had never cared. But now, it seemed bitter that Mother would still have to pay to support a church she no longer attended.

And of course Mother had sacrificed friends. But she was thrilled and excited about her new acquaintances. It was, "Mima, did I tell you Sister Midgley also enjoys Berlin work?" Or, "Mima, Sister Woolley sang the most beautiful hymn tonight at meeting. I shall have her write down the score for you." And now these new friends had gathered to watch as Mother was baptized in this godforsaken brook.

I had not promised to sacrifice friends, but what of Charlotte? We had grown together in ruffles and bonnets. She had been as dear to me as any sister, yet now there was an unbreachable distance. Last week she had glanced away when I reached for her hand at choir rehearsal, moving to the other side of the room to avoid me. More than ever before, I longed to share some of this pain. But few words had passed between us then or since. Only frozen silence.

The Mormons sang a hymn I was not familiar with. The singers were clearly untrained. Though the song itself was pleasant enough, performed in the open air, the hymn sounded impossibly out of place. Without the lovely stone arches, the sound was snatched, lost, torn away by the wind. It had none of the resonance of church music, none of the reverence. Like fragments of notes flung across a farmer's field.

A Mormon man used a hatchet to break the ice. The hatchet split through that cold protective layer, shivering it to pieces. The sound was beautiful, a kind of fragile music, playing in my ears as the barrier sheared away. The man wielding the hatchet was winded from the effort, his thick muscles swelling through his coat, his breath puffing out in circles as he worked. My mother waited in white upon white.

I thought again about Elder Russell's words: "Sacrifice everything." Even family. That meant that if Mother had to choose, she could not choose me. She would sacrifice me on the altar of this strange new religion. I shivered.

Elder Russell removed his hat and coat and handed them to another Mormon nearby. His jaw muscles flinched as the wind blew through him. He beckoned to Mother. "Sister Hough, it is time."

Mother removed her hat, revealing her gray hair, which she had secured in a bun. She was not smiling now. She approached the dark, swirling water hesitantly.

Elder Russell entered the water, his teeth clenching against the shock.

Mother paused.

Elder Russell said, "Take faith, Sister Hough."

Mother closed her eyes for a moment and then opened them and stepped strongly into the water. The dusky water swallowed up her boots and dragged at her dress, swirling white against black. She moved deeper into the water, her breath coming faster as the impact of the cold water registered. Her lips began to tremble.

But she bowed her head, and Elder Russell raised his arm, his fingertips pointing to the stony layer of clouds. "Jemima Drabwell Rushby Hough," he began. I was captured by the look on my mother's face, her gray eyes closed. On her face was a look of—I did not know the word—perhaps it was peace: like a soft summer day; it was joy, quiet and still; and more than anything it was sturdy: strong enough to hold onto.

"I baptize you in the name of the Father and of the Son and of the Holy Ghost. Amen." With a quick movement, Elder Russell dipped my mother into the water. For a brief moment she disappeared, swallowed up in the inky waves without a trace. Then she was back, coughing, sputtering, smiling, and crying—climbing out of the water. They descended on her, those new Mormon friends, wrapped her in blanket after blanket, dabbed the water from her hair.

I stood back, watching them help her, with nothing to offer.

But she turned to me anyway. "My Mima," she said and embraced me. "I am thankful you came." Her hug was warm, yet icy water dripped onto my cloak and soaked through my gloves. I shivered and hugged her back, loving her even as I hated her.

My mother was baptized. Again. And suddenly I knew what I had seen on her face—that look, that expression, the feeling that had wrung me to my core. It was *knowing*.

CHAPTER SEVEN

A week later, Mother and I set out for our weekly walk to St. Margaret's. I was in a dark mood and took little care to hide it.

"How was your rehearsal?" asked Mother.

"Effective," I said.

She looked at me with a sidelong glance, but I kept my eyes on the road ahead. I knew she wondered how Charlotte and the others were treating me. But I did not wish to discuss it with her. It was her fault, after all.

"Do you like the songs you are learning with Miss Pritchard?" she asked.

"Well enough," I replied.

I glanced at the sky, wishing this walk were over. The sky was gray and pasty, as if a large wool quilt had been draped over the heavens. We walked along the edge of the moors, where patches of bracken and heather poked between the snowdrifts.

Usually I enjoyed visiting Father's grave, late on Sunday afternoons when regular services were over. St. Margaret's was actually closer to Providence House than to St. Peter's. St. Margaret's was where my parents had been married and where Father's ancestors back through generations were buried. Yet Mother and I never went there when other people might be present. It was too risky.

"We need to finish the lace caps for Miss Gregory," Mother said.

"We will have plenty of time tomorrow," I said, lifting my skirts to avoid a patch of frozen mud on the road. "I know of few other orders that need to be done."

Mother pursed her thin lips and grew silent at last. I felt a twinge of guilt but was glad of the silence. We neared St. Margaret's, and I spied the graveyard. The sun shone just enough to cast shadows— sooty shadows that spilled over the stone box graves. Bits of dead leaves tucked among the piles of dirty snow littered the ground. Some of the headstones had begun to tip with time—some tipped to the right, others to the left. They looked dizzy, as if they had been surprised when the solid ground gave way beneath them.

Mother and I went to Father's monument, the most prominent in the churchyard, directly outside the main steps. The single edifice held two plaques, entwined together. On the first, "In memory of Ann, wife of William Hough, who died June 25th, 1832. What a wife and mother should be, she was to her children and me." On the second, "Sacred to the memory of William Hough. Blessed are the dead which die in the Lord." The headstone was complete, finished, husband and wife resting side by side, with no room for my mother.

Mother pressed her fingers to the stone. I had done that many times. I was four years old when Father was buried here. A few snatches of memories and a melody without words were all I had of my father. But in this graveyard I had spent many hours imagining him, trying to understand this person who gave me my height and my wide-set brown eyes. I had talked to the stone, coaxed it, caressed it. Tried to recall his voice, his scent, his mannerisms. But it had never worked. As much as I tried, I had never been able to get the stone to show me my father.

Mother closed her eyes and leaned into the stone, as if asking it for strength. "Mima, we are going to have to leave," she said.

Shock ran through me. "What do you mean?"

Mother opened her eyes but still leaned against the stone. I began to wonder if it was holding her up. "We are losing customers, one by one. Soon we will not have anything left. We cannot stay here."

"Where can we go?" I suddenly felt like the tipsy tombstones, reeling with shock.

"We can sell Providence House to your father's daughter. She has always wanted it. I will take you to Liverpool to live with George. It is a large city. You will be able to study music, as you have longed to. Your brother and his wife will be kind."

Liverpool. I couldn't imagine leaving Wooden Box, and yet the idea of studying music in a city left me speechless with joy. Suddenly leaving seemed like the only solution—of course we could leave the coldness and cruelty of this place. "Will they accept Mormons in Liverpool?"

"I'm sure they will be more accepting in a city like Liverpool," said Mother. "It takes more to shock a large city than a little village like Wooden Box. But that will hardly matter to you, after all."

"But of course it will," I said, and then fear darted into my mind. "Will we *both* go to Liverpool?"

Mother cleared her throat, pressing her hand against the stone again. "I have thought about it a great deal, Mima. And I think it would be best if I go to Zion. I will settle with the Mormons."

"You will leave me?" I asked. I sat down hard on the cold steps of the church. "You promised you wouldn't leave me."

Mother's eyes filled with tears. At last she left the gravestone and came to sit beside me.

"Dear Mima," she said, "I do not want to leave you. But I cannot abide the thought of being a burden to anyone. And you will be better off with George and Sarah. They are well connected. They will offer you a good life."

She took my hand, and her gloves were chilled.

"I want to go to Liverpool," I said. "I want to study music. But I want you to stay."

"George and Sarah would never permit a Mormon to stay," said Mother at last.

"Then why do you have to *be* a Mormon?" I asked.

Mother sighed. "Mima, at times I wish that I did not have to be a Mormon."

I caught my breath. Perhaps now she would tell me about the mind-altering.

"But I must," she continued. "I know what the Mormons preach is right. I know it is true. I cannot pretend that I do not know."

I wanted to stuff my fingers in my ears like a little child.

"But that doesn't mean I need to ruin your promising life. You will be better off with George and Sarah."

"I will be better off without a mother?" I looked at her incredulously. "I will be an orphan with Father in this graveyard and you across the sea." My chest was a tight knot of pain.

"You are too young to understand what you would be sacrificing if you came with me," said Mother. "You are fourteen now, but soon you will be thinking about your future. I cannot ruin your prospects."

She wept, and I was glad she was crying, because I could not. The pain in my chest was too great. I leaned into the stone steps and tried to keep breathing.

A memory darted into my head. Another visit to the graveyard when I had not been careful enough. Mrs. Harrison had found me touching Father's headstone, just as Mother had been doing. Mrs. Harrison, my half-sister by blood, but not a sister in any real sense of the word. I saw in her eyes the pain that I caused her by the simple fact I existed. She wanted to pretend my parents' marriage had not occurred one year and one day after her mother's death, that her father had not fallen in love with a woman three years younger than his own son.

Mrs. Harrison sneered when she saw me. "Oh, how nice. You have come to pay respects to my parents," she said.

"To my father," I replied.

"I didn't know you still visited this place. Your parents were married for such a short time, and as you hardly knew him, I would not expect you to visit."

"He was my father, Mrs. Harrison, just as he was yours."

"How dare you compare your relationship with him to mine? They are not remotely similar."

And I knew then that nothing I could say could convince her, because she was right. Our relationships were not remotely similar. She had been raised by him. She had years of memories. All I had was a graveyard. What would I have if Mother left? I would not have a graveyard. I would have memories. And letters, of course. Which would be better? A place or a memory? I wanted a parent.

I pulled my hand from Mother's and moved to the headstone. Each breath was painful. I tugged off a glove. My father's name, carved in the stone, felt cool beneath my hand. "Good-bye, Father," I whispered. He had been a wool carder in his youth, then a tenant farmer, and finally a man who owned sanitary potteries and could build a house as grand as Providence House. But all I remembered were his strong arms carrying me up to my room, long past my bedtime, cradled against his chest as his rich, bass voice hummed a melody, haunting and mournful. A song without words. A sound that resonated deep inside his chest. Such a warm, safe sound.

Mother huddled on the church steps, looking frail and old. How could she travel over the ocean in search of Zion? I thought of the white city I had pictured at Evensong. *It can't be real,* I thought.

As I pressed my fingers again to the stone and whispered one last time, "Good-bye, Father," I felt the stone reproving me for letting my mother cross the ocean alone.

"She is leaving me. I am not leaving her," I told the curling letters. But the stone was cold and unforgiving beneath my hands, and I heard the rocky reproof continue just the same.

CHAPTER EIGHT

When the knock came, echoing through Providence House, it was as if the walls picked up the sound and shouted it along. As I heard Martha move to answer this strange knock so late in the evening, my mind was blank. Who could it be? A customer?

I moved silently to the entryway, covered in shadows, and peeked around the corner before Martha announced the visitor. Under a wet and wind-blown cloak was a face I knew well. "Charlotte," I said, my heart skipping. I had not seen her alone since Evensong several weeks before.

As I looked at her face, a decade of memories passed before me: hunting for wild mushrooms along the road to Blackfordby, pretending to be sisters; wandering ankle deep in bilberries; working figures on our slates at the desk we shared in school; exploring Ashby Castle, where we made up stories of haunts and fairies that lived among the ancient stones; and, of course, singing together. How many songs had we sung together?

I tumbled into the entryway. Martha looked from my face to Charlotte's, curtseyed, and disappeared.

"You came," I said, my pulse loud in my ears.

"Just for a moment," she said. She looked distinctly out of place and glanced nervously at the door.

I felt a sharp sliver of pain. Providence House had once been her second home. "My mother does not know I'm here," she said.

We entered the parlor. As she had so many times before, Charlotte sat down on the horsehair divan. Her cloak was still on, but a few wet curls sprang from the corners.

I sat next to her, and she pressed my hand.

"Here I am breaking rules once again for you, Mima." Her dimples danced, and for a moment, it seemed as if nothing had changed between us.

I smiled. "Truly I am a bad influence on you, Charlotte. Your mother has always said so. Little does she know your golden curls hide a black and rebellious heart." I leaned close to my friend. "Yet I seem to remember that it was your idea to throw plums at Mrs. Flaim."

Charlotte giggled. "Only because you had convinced me that she was a witch."

I smiled. "You must admit she was suspicious."

"You filled my head with such stories," said Charlotte. She laughed again, and then her face grew serious. She clasped my hand, looking deep into my eyes. "And now, are you truly leaving, Mima?"

Even though I had been over this in my head a thousand times and I thought leaving was what I truly wanted—and even though I thought I was used to the idea—when Charlotte asked, the pain and shock were like the first time Mother told me in the graveyard. It threw me into turmoil all over again. Did we *really* have to leave?

"Yes," I said at last. The breath caught in my chest, but I pushed emotion away. "Mother is going to America, and I am going to stay with George and Sarah in Liverpool."

"However will you bear to be away from her?" Charlotte's eyes were open and kind, the eyes of a friend who has known you for as long as you can remember.

But she and I were no longer the friends we once had been. My voice was raw and wary. "I will study music. George and Sarah are lovely. And as for Wooden Box . . . there is little to keep us here."

Charlotte winced. "I am sorry people have been unkind."

"I wouldn't expect more from this backwards little village. People are afraid of what they do not understand." I tried to swallow the lump in my throat. "But I did not think they would also be able to persuade you."

"I am sorry," she said. "You don't know what people have been saying. What Mother has been saying." She sighed. "But I came tonight. I came to say good-bye and to bring you this." From her cloak she drew a small silk purse. She set it on the table.

I stared at it blankly. "What is it?" I asked.

"It is mine to give, a small part of what will be my inheritance. Mother does not know, but Grandfather said I was free to give it to you if I chose. You do not know what is ahead of you in this journey."

"Please," I said. Tears pricked my eyes, tears that after all these weeks she would come at last, when I was ready to leave everything behind. "Don't be silly. We will be fine."

"You have been a sister to me," she said. "I will not have it back. It is a fraction of what you should have had from your father's inheritance. Think of it as a gift from him." She was on her feet, ready to leave.

I picked up the purse and held it out to her. "Take the purse, Charlotte. It is not mine."

She crossed the room and turned back at the door. Her eyes were pleading. "It is yours, and I beg you not to return it. I would not send my sister to Liverpool alone. I will imagine you in Liverpool, studying music. Think of me when you sing. And perhaps . . . write to me." She returned to kiss my cheek, and I smelled lavender. Then she slipped out the door, swallowed up in the black, frosty night, leaving me alone in the doorway with the wind blowing through me and the feel of silk upon my fingers. I turned away from the door, opened the purse, and counted the coins. Twenty-five guineas. So much money. Enough to take me to the New World and back again. Why did she think I would need this? *Would* I need it?

I heard a footstep behind me. I turned quickly, thrusting the purse behind my back. Mother's eyebrows were knotted in concern. "Was that Charlotte?"

"Yes," I said, my face flushed.

"What did she want?"

"To say good-bye." I kept my back to the door. I hardly knew why I hid the purse from her, but I did not want her to know.

Mother's face was kind, and I felt a pinch of guilt for deceiving her. "I am glad she came, Mima. She was a dear friend."

I nodded. *Was* a dear friend. Pain sliced through me, swift and sure. I buried the purse deeper still.

CHAPTER NINE

*T*he coach sent by George rattled up the road and stopped in front of Providence House. I watched it come, leaning heavily against the window of my bedroom. In a daze, I watched it drive up, and part of me wondered, "Who will ride in that coach?" I wanted to wait and see what hands would grip the door and sweep aside the curtain to watch as the little town of Wooden Box—with its cottages, toll booth, and potteries—fell off in the distance.

I turned back to my room, my lovely room with yellow paper and crisp white draperies: it was dismantled, taken apart at the seams and sucked into a trunk, sitting in the middle of the floor, into which I had packed clippings of roses and all the blossoms I loved best (I could not fit the garden), clothes and necessities and books (it would not hold the window seat where I read them). With all that I had packed, there was so much I could not take: the furniture that had been in Father's family for generations; the smell of cabbage roses on a summer evening as the stars came out one by one; the afternoon sunshine that floated in the white-trimmed windows and danced on the mirrors in the hall.

I heard the tinkling sound of Mother's chatelaine before she tapped on the door. "Your scores are still on the pianoforte," she said.

"Yes, I'll get them."

She nodded. "I'll send the footman for your trunk, then." She smiled and left the room. How could she smile at a time like this? She had been smiling for several days now, and it made me feel slightly sick. As the departure drew nearer, I could see that Mother was actually happy about leaving Wooden Box. Of course I knew she loved Providence House differently from the way I loved it—she had moved here as a bride, and I had been born here. But I had never realized that she had slowly grown to despise the house she once loved.

Suddenly I realized that she would have left right after my father died, except . . . except for me. She had stayed for my sake, because as long as she stayed, there was hope that she would receive the money from Father's estate, which would have been a dowry. She had stayed, although we never received the money. I saw that she truly loved me, and here was proof—it had taken years for her to leave this place that for her had become a wooden box of grief.

And yet this was the most beautiful place on earth to me. I felt a shiver of fear. The place in which I was happiest, she was not. And yet her sewing room was torturous to me. We were so different. Perhaps regardless of the Mormons, we needed an ocean between us.

I went downstairs to retrieve the scores. Mother had worried I would forget them, but of course I had not. I had saved them for last, because taking them meant I was really leaving. I stood next to the pianoforte and began to stack the scores in a pile. But when I had finished, I could not turn away. I did not care if a dozen coaches were waiting. I settled onto the bench and ran my fingers across the carved cherry casing, along the ivory keys. The keys, as always, marched up the keyboard in perfect order. Three black keys, then two, then three, and two, and three again. Over and over, all the way up the keyboard. Steady. Ordered. Dependable.

I remembered music lessons, which at first in my fumbling had little to do with music. I learned the scales; I played the melodies Miss Pritchard asked me to play. Then one day, sick of my spiritless plunking, she said, "Hush, child. Listen to what I am trying to teach you." And she began to play the most beautiful song I had ever heard, a song that made me think of fairies skipping over the flowers as moonlight danced around. I listened, breathless, for I had not known that the instrument was capable of such sound. When Miss Pritchard was finished, when I saw her fingers curl and lift from the keys, I finally let out my breath.

"Please, Miss Pritchard," I breathed. "Please tell me what they call that song?"

"'Moonlight' Sonata, child."

I knew at that moment that I wanted to do nothing but make

honey-tasting music on the pianoforte and sing those same glorious notes with my throat, so that I could be filled with the music, that it might pass through me, leaving some of the sweetness behind.

Now my fingers moved of their own accord. They played a Mozart minuet. Light and airy, as out of place as Mother's smile. But if I played my real emotions, I was afraid the dam inside would burst, and my sorrow would smash all over the pianoforte. When I was finished, my fingers lifted slowly, so slowly from the keys. I leaned across the keys, as if to embrace them.

Then I gathered the scores, looked one last time at the pianoforte, and walked back to my room, each step pulling at my heart. "May I carry those for you, miss?" Martha asked, as I struggled up the stairs.

"No, thank you, Martha," I said. "I've got them." I wrapped the scores with string and placed them beside my overflowing trunk. The trunk was pitifully small. It could never hold half of what I wanted to take with me. I glanced out the window at the horses pawing, their breath rising in the air, anxious to be off. The driver was pacing, fists thrust into his coat for warmth. I sighed and told myself firmly, "The coach is here for me."

CHAPTER TEN

I tried not to cry as we drove away from Providence House. Martha sobbed into her handkerchief and waved until we were out of sight. We clattered past the shops on High Street, where ladies in bonnets and parasols strolled as ever, and men had their hair trimmed and their horses shod just like any other day. I clenched my hands until they ached. We rattled past the potteries that had made Father his fortune. I blinked fiercely. Then we turned a corner. I had hoped we would not go this way. We passed in front of Charlotte's home, still frosted with snow about the eaves. Behind the curtains, shadows moved, Charlotte and her parents sitting down to tea perhaps. They were speaking of the weather or discussing the day's plans, plans that would never include me.

I could hold the pain no longer. I leaned my head against the window of the carriage and let the tears slide down my cheeks. Mother cried along with me, but it seemed like it was mostly to keep me company. She cried the tears people feel obligated to shed when their lives change. I was sure that underneath her tears, her grief was not as deep as mine. The rattle of the carriage drowned out the noise.

As we traveled, the cottages stretched farther apart, interspersed with bare trees and frozen meadows, the road bordered by a crumbling rock wall. Then we passed through the bustling towns of Swadlincote and Burton-on-Trent, and we were in Derbyshire, farther west than I had ever been in my whole life. Soon the cottages and rock walls disappeared, and we were passing through wild land—broad moors and rocky crags, tumbling rivers and deep forest. The land was wild and rich and free.

An eerie feeling came over me. As the land changed, I knew I would soon be changing too. I was traveling far beyond the places I had seen before. My life was going to be different from the one I had always planned for, and perhaps I would become someone I would not otherwise be. I felt my heart stretched out in new directions, all achy and sore from the reaching.

The rattle of the coach made speaking impossible, but after many hours, we stopped at an inn called the Bull's Head. To leave behind the cold rocking of the coach for a warm fire, hot tea, and a soft bed was heavenly. Mother and I ate the inn meal: steak and kidney pie, suet pudding, and watercress. As we ate I asked, "Do you think I will like George?"

Mother sighed. "You know him yourself."

"Hardly," I replied. "I was a child when he left for Liverpool. I have seen him only a Christmas or two since then."

Mother rubbed her eyes. We were both exhausted, but curiosity about my half-brother kept my eyes open.

"Very well," she said. She was quiet for a moment, but I knew her well enough to know that she had not forgotten. Her brain was sorting and organizing the information. When it was arranged correctly, she would relay it. This was something that amused me about Mother. I loved it and laughed at it, though sometimes it caused me annoyance. But regardless, I knew I could never cause her to answer quickly. She was prone to sew a seam ten times until it met her satisfaction, lying flat and even—just so. Many times I wished I could be more that way, cool and methodical. My tendency to blurt out my opinions had gotten me into trouble more than once.

"It is strange," she said at last, "that your half-brother, George, is like me in many ways, but even more so." She smiled. "So little like you and your father. He is neat, punctual, and disciplined. A merchant's clerk with a clear, steady hand and a swift head for figures."

"Even more so?"

"Well, yes. We both appreciate order, but George is so logical he barely seems aware of emotions."

I grimaced. "How will he tolerate me? I shall torture him."

"George will adore you," said Mother. "Just as you are good for me, so you will be good for him."

"And what will you do, Mother, without someone to help you with disorganization?" My voice was teasing, my face a smile.

But Mother's eyes were solemn and serious. "I hardly know." Her voice was rough.

My smile faded. I thought of the last time I had seen George. Christmas at Providence House. The spicy scent of the Christmas tree, laced with strings of cranberries, popcorn, and paper flowers. The taste of plum puddings, the sound of the carols. I remembered George, reserved and solemn, yet kind, and Sarah, shy and ill at ease with her husband's family. I was going to live with them. Spend Christmas with them—every Christmas from now on. Without Mother. My head hummed.

But I tried to coax a smile from her by saying, "I will send you letters that invite you to do impulsive, irrational acts."

Mother squeezed my hand as if she would never let go.

I was exhausted from our journey and thought I would be asleep as soon as I lay down upon my pillow. And yet I tossed and turned upon the stiffly starched sheets, waking several times disoriented, without a memory of where I was. I missed my bed at Providence House. I lay awake and stared at the strange shadows cast by furniture that was not my own.

Oddly, I ached for my father. I could not remember his face, but I wanted his arms to hold me close, and I wanted his voice to tell me it would be all right, that he would take care of us. But all I saw was the Blackfordby graveyard: my fingers pressed to Father's headstone, his voice chiding me because my mother would cross an ocean alone.

CHAPTER ELEVEN

I dozed in the coach, as cold and noisy as it was, while it drew ever closer to Liverpool. First the hamlets were closer together, then there were the large towns of Prescot and Warrington, and then quite suddenly we could see the hazy outline of hundreds of factories in the distance, their smoke stacks belching black smoke into the air. We descended into the city and found a tumult I never had imagined: Liverpool. I could not take in the rush of it—carriages racing this way and that, fancy traps, and even an omnibus, double-decked and pulled by two strong horses. I reached for Mother's arm, and we exclaimed over it together.

Mother pointed to the cobbled streets and sidewalks. I tugged on her arm at the sight of the gas street lamps. We passed Liverpool

Cathedral, with a central tower and spires so high I thought the building would surely tip over. Each building seemed grander than the last—until finally we came to St. George's Plateau. Vast scaffolds and levers were raising a stony spire that sprang toward the sky, and the hulking mass of St. George's Hall was rising from the square. I had never imagined any place so grand.

The Salvation Army was having a march near the Plateau, with a banner and marching band. The noise of the city was overwhelming—the churning of the factories, the motion of thousands of horses and carts, the humanity, alive and surging past me. The smells were ferocious—the black, stifling smell of factories, the putrid stench of overflowing privies, the smell of too many people living on top of each other. Mother pressed her handkerchief to her nose.

We turned off the main road onto a narrower street, and the coach came to a stop. Suddenly shadows moved in the blackness of a darkened alleyway. The shadows came toward us, and finally I realized the huddled figures were people—a woman and three scrawny children, their bodies filthy, their feet bare, their clothing rags. The children were pitiful wretches, the mother's face framed with black and matted hair. "Please, miss," she said, moving to the coach, "spare a penny for the young 'uns?" I stared at her in utter horror. My hands flew to my bag, fumbling for a coin, but before I could open it, the carriage started forward again, and she was left behind in the dirt of the alley.

I tugged open the small window that separated us from the driver. "We must turn back!" I said. "That woman needs help! Driver! Please turn back."

"Aw, miss," he replied, "no use givin' her your money. No offense, but her husband would probably jus' drink it all. I know it's a bit of a shock the first time you see 'em, but there's hundreds here just like her, all of 'em in want of a coin."

I sank back to my seat. Mother took my hand. I wasn't sure if she was comforting me or seeking her own comfort. I could not erase the vivid lines of that woman's face, the intense need, the desperate suffering. Did she sleep on that cold, black street? Huddled with those miserable children for warmth? A warm bed and fire awaited us. There in the carriage, I cried for Wooden Box, where everyone I knew had a room to sleep in. And I cried because I had come to a strange and smoky city where mothers and little filthy children could starve on the streets and no one seemed to care. I sobbed, and the whole time Mother just held onto my hand and said, "Shh, Mima."

"Number 19 Water Street," the driver said at last. He alighted and placed the steps for our descent. I wiped my face, and we stepped onto the cobbled sidewalks of Liverpool. A servant answered our knock, and then Sarah and George came to greet us. Sarah's honey-colored hair was arranged in fashionable coils, and the skirts of her gray silk receiving dress were cut in a style I had never seen before. George was resplendent in a charcoal waistcoat and dangling gold pocket watch. He looked older than when I had seen him last—he was a fashionable man, with sideburns and a peppered mustache. My half-brother. I suddenly felt dusty and old-fashioned in my brown wool traveling suit.

"Mother. Mima." George embraced us each in turn. I thought perhaps he would brush his clothing after touching us, but he did not.

"Welcome," said Sarah. "Please come in." We entered a small drawing room decorated with peach and gold damask draperies where tea, sandwiches, and sweet cakes were waiting. I noticed the carved walnut pianoforte in a corner of the room and eyed it longingly.

When we were settled, Sarah remarked, "What a journey you must have had. Imagine—the two of you traveling all alone!"

"Mima and I are accustomed to being alone," Mother said. George and Sarah exchanged a glance.

"Sarah forgets how capable you are," said George. "Most women would not be willing to contemplate such a journey without a man's protection. But you are used to such situations."

"Yes, we are," said Mother. "Mima and I do very well."

George cleared his throat. "And what do you think of our Liverpool? Is she not grand? She is the fastest growing city in England. We are the center of the manufacturing world."

"Liverpool is grand," said Mother. "I have never seen anything like it."

George stroked his mustache. "Fortunes are being made in the factories of this city. 'The workshop of the world,' they call us."

Sarah arranged her skirts, and I noticed the flash of gold on her finger. "George likes to remember the factories, but this is also a great center for society, too. Mima may choose between several seminaries for young women, all of them acclaimed for turning out fine ladies."

"And musical instruction?" I asked. My eyes returned to the pianoforte.

"Oh, yes," she replied, "music is taught along with the other

important arts: French, elocution, painting, poise, and needlework."
She smiled at Mother. "Although I daresay you need little training in
the latter."

George made an impatient gesture. "Mother, Liverpool needs a talented seamstress. Sarah and I would like to convince you to stay here.
Are you still determined to continue your journey?"

The late afternoon sun passed through Sarah's open damask draperies and lit up Mother's hair—peppered gray. Mother looked from
George to me and back again. Finally she said, "Yes, I am determined
to continue. I know it is best if I go, even though it pains me. I feel
peaceful, even while my heart breaks."

"Mother, you and I do not speak the same language when you talk
of feelings and hearts. I prefer a more logical approach. I fear your letters from across the Atlantic will speak of hardship," said George.

"Perhaps," said Mother. "But I want to settle with others who believe as I do and help build Zion. I know this course of action is best,
although it may be difficult."

I know this. There were those words again. How could Mother
claim to know the future? I did not understand her certainty. It frightened me. Perhaps because my own feelings changed with such regular-
ity, the thought of knowing future feelings seemed alarming.

George stood up and paced the room. Sarah cleared her throat.
"My love, all the world is not facts and figures. Your mother has decided, and we must wish her safety in her journey."

I looked from George to Mother. I was slightly dazzled by his poise and wondered how Mother could remain firm in the face of his cool logic and elegance.

But he nodded to Sarah and said, "You are right. Forgive me, Mother. I desire only your safety."

"The Lord will protect me," she said.

That didn't seem to reassure George, and he shrugged impatiently.

Sarah leaned forward to take my hand. "You must have crossed the Plateau? No matter how often I see it, I am always amazed by the grandeur that is being created there."

I turned to her, relieved to change the subject. "I have never imagined a building so enormous as it will be," I confessed. "But . . . as we turned away from the square, I saw a mother and three wretched children. They looked horribly hungry."

"Street urchins," said George. "They are filthy. Spread disease and crime."

"Why doesn't someone help them?" I asked. "They need food."

"People like that cannot be helped," said George. "They exist in every city, and they will always exist. They cannot be helped."

But the mother's face, her desperate eyes, were seared into my mind. And although I heard my brother's words and saw the confidence on his face, still I did not believe him.

CHAPTER TWELVE

hortly after breakfast Mother asked Sarah for the carriage. Soon we were clattering through the streets of Liverpool on the way to the home of Reuben Bradshaw, the Mormon emigration agent. He lived quite close to the waterfront, and the closer we got to the water, the worse the smells grew. Once again I smelled the privies, this time mingled with a foul smell that could only come from slaughterhouses. The streets were crowded with more beggars like the woman I had seen as we entered Liverpool. They spoke with an Irish brogue, and I realized they were victims of the famine in their own country. Could life in Ireland really be more horrible than living on Liverpool's streets? I remembered Rector Buckley saying that Ireland's famine was God's punishment on the Catholics. How could this suffering be the work of God? I saw one woman squatting beside the road, feeding a baby from her bare, dirty breast. Although I had coins ready, I gave very few, afraid the people would swarm the coach.

We came at last to the docks. Magnificent walls of masonry stretched before us, vast piers of granite that seemed to hold the very sea at bay. Beyond the estuary of the River Mersey was the ocean. I had never seen it. There it lay like a thing alive—tossing and shifting, a myriad of colors and tints playing through the swells. Attached to the granite-rimmed docks were ships so large they seemed to blot out the sky. Crowds of people rushed this way and that, loading and unloading bales of cotton, tobacco, grain, boxes, parcels, and raw materials arriving to be worked in Liverpool's famous factories.

Mother eyed the large ships carefully, and I realized with a start that she would soon be on a boat like these, heading over the endless sea. I shuddered and gripped her hand more tightly.

When the coach stopped, we were handed off in front of a brick row house.

"Sister Hough," Brother Bradshaw said, entering the room with a bow and a jolly smile. I started at hearing my mother so addressed and then remembered this was the Mormon custom. "Welcome to Liverpool."

He turned to me. "And you must be Miss Jemima." I nodded. "I am Brother Bradshaw. You are most welcome. How do you find Liverpool?"

I looked from his smiling face to Mother's steady gray eyes, unsure how to respond. "In all honesty, Brother Bradshaw, I have found Liverpool to be quite . . . overwhelming," I said.

"To be sure, miss, 'tis that. It's a sad state things are in, and with more victims of the famine arriving daily, things are getting worse, I'm afraid. Still," he said, pulling on the end of his mustache, "we try to assist."

"You are helping them?" I asked.

He looked at me in surprise. "We set up public baths, shelter, and food; we try to help them find employment. The problem is there are just too many. But we help as many as we can."

I was impressed, in spite of my resolve not to be.

He nodded. "And now, Sister Hough, you must be anxious to know about your passage." He went to a desk, opened it, and withdrew several papers. "You are booked on a vessel named the *Parthenon*. You will be quite comfortable. It will depart on Friday with the morning tide, so you may board anytime tomorrow evening. All seems in order. Although," he paused and checked the paper again, his brow furrowed. "It says here there is passage for only one. A mere oversight. Adding your daughter will be no trouble."

Mother stared at the papers in Brother Bradshaw's hands. "My daughter will not be accompanying me, sir. She is to remain in Liverpool."

Brother Bradshaw looked up in surprise. "Oh, I see," he said, as if it were the most natural thing in the world. "I assure you, Sister Hough, we take excellent care of our passengers. You will encounter no trouble traveling alone on a Mormon ship." He turned to me, and his eyes were two blue question marks. But he said only, "Miss Jemima, our city is honored to welcome you."

Mother gathered her shawl to leave, but Brother Bradshaw stopped her. "And now I have a small gift for you. I won't be a moment." He hurried from the room. Mother and I exchanged quizzical glances. He returned with a book in each hand. He carried them extended slightly from his body as if to keep them safe.

"First, a gift for you, Sister Hough," he said, and placed a narrow volume in Mother's hands. I leaned close to her so that I could watch her open the black leather cover and read the title page: THE BOOK OF MORMON: AN ACCOUNT WRITTEN BY THE HAND OF MORMON, UPON PLATES TAKEN FROM THE PLATES OF NEPHI . . . BY JOSEPH SMITH, JUNIOR.

Mother gasped and held the book away from her, just as Brother Bradshaw had done. "I have seen it only a few times," she said. "To hold it in my hands—this journey was small inconvenience for such a prize."

I felt my mother's joy and surprise, even though I did not share her emotion. I had heard much about this book, though few Mormons in Wooden Box had a copy. The gold bible, which Joseph Smith had supposedly found buried in the ground and translated with God's help. It looked so small and unassuming, just like any other book. Hardly large enough to wrench families apart.

But now Brother Bradshaw turned to me. "For you, my dear," he said. "These copies just arrived, and although we usually sell them, I would like to make a gift of this one." He handed me an even smaller book, bound in brown leather.

I wondered what to do. Should I tell him I was not a Mormon? Would it be rude to decline this gift? Hesitant, I took the book and turned to the title page, and this time Mother looked over my shoulder as I read: *A Collection of Sacred Hymns, for the Church of Jesus Christ of Latter-Day Saints, in Europe.* A hymnal. How could this man possibly know this was the one gift I would accept? I looked up at him, still unsure of what to do, saw his smile, and knew I could not refuse. "Thank you," I said and was surprised to find I meant it.

We left his home with Mother's papers and the books tucked firmly in her bag. I paused on the steps. I could sense the ocean not far away, simmering in the distance. I felt the creaking timbers of a ship, the *Parthenon,* ready to carry my mother across that rocking deep. And I heard my father's voice, speaking from a stone: "How can you leave her alone?"

CHAPTER THIRTEEN

*T*he day slipped away like sand down a steep shore. "Come and say good-bye to your mother, Mima." Mother's voice rang out too sharp, too soon. I rushed to her arms, enfolded by the softness of her, the lemon of her dress sachets and something else, impossible to define, that made the fragrance hers alone.

"Farewell," she said.

"Don't leave me."

"I must go before the ship sails," she said.

I clung to her, trying to memorize her embrace.

"Mima, it will make me happy knowing that you will be able to receive the training you deserve. Study diligently. Sing for me."

"I will."

"I love you," she said. I tried to echo the phrase but found the words jumbled by tears.

"Write to me."

I nodded.

She bade farewell to Sarah and George, and then she was gone, trunk and parcels stowed on the coach. I watched the coach disappear down the street as tears streamed down my face. Sarah stood beside me, her arm around my shoulders for comfort. The coach was quickly swallowed up by the crowded street. Emotions struggled within me, and I hardly knew what I felt.

I turned back to the house and wandered from room to room like a lonely bird. George and Sarah tried desperately to engage me. Sarah prattled about the seminaries, about the concert halls of the city. George cleared his throat and tried to think of something to say. After several times around the room, my feet stopped at last before the pianoforte.

"Oh, do play for us, Mima," Sarah entreated. "We have not heard you play."

George nodded, although at that moment it did not matter to me if they wanted me to play or not. I was hardly conscious of their presence.

The pianoforte was an anchor in the room, solid and sturdy. I sat. Here at last, my fingers found something familiar. I closed my eyes, sensing the shapes of the keys. With my eyes closed I could pretend I was home. I began to play. Bach for my brother. The rhythms precise, each note just so. Order, serenity, exactness flowing from my hands.

But after a time I moved to Beethoven's "Moonlight" Sonata. As I played, my emotions quieted and fell into place. There, in that familiar space, I began to sort through my feelings.

The deep, rolling chords of the left hand became a dark, tempestuous sea. I was lost in the cadence, pulling me under. The strong, repeated high notes in the right hand seemed imploring. "Come to me," they seemed to say. The song became a battleground. I pressed the keys so hard the muscles of my fingers ached. Deeper and deeper I fell into the bottomless melody. As the song ended, my finger clung to the final note, resonant and true. A longing struggled up from the murky depths of the song. Mother was all that was left of Father. Mother was all that was left of home.

I must go with her, I thought and knew at once that it was true. Horror and calm coursed through me all at the same time.

I looked up. George and Sarah were staring at me with open mouths as if they were wondering what had happened to their pianoforte. "I must go with her," I said aloud.

George closed his mouth and tugged impatiently at his cravat. "Oh, Mima. Think of what awaits you here. Don't follow Mother's ridiculous dream."

What he said was true enough. All my life I had dreamed of the kind of musical training Liverpool offered. I yearned for that opportunity, but I still shivered with the clarity I had felt as I played. "I am sorry, but I must go with her. I can't let her go alone. I must leave at once." My fingers lingered on the pianoforte keys, reluctant to leave the reassurance of their safety.

"Are you certain that is what you want?" Sarah asked. Her eyes were worried.

I nodded.

"Very well," said George with a sigh. "I fear you will find nothing but sorrow in the New World, but if you must go, we will help you."

I arose from the pianoforte, and a load of worries beset me. How would I find Mother? Would the ship have space for me? I had packed for a life in Liverpool, not an early spring at sea. What would we find in America? I pushed these thoughts away and focused on finding my hat and gloves. George called for another coach. Sarah had the cook wrap up a bundle of cheese and bread.

An hour later, I climbed into a coach loaded with all my earthly possessions and departed from the house on Water Street. George paid the driver and told him to take me to the *Parthenon*, instructing him to remain with me. As I waved farewell to George and Sarah, my hands shook uncontrollably, and I could only wonder if I had just thrown to the wind all that was precious to me.

CHAPTER FOURTEEN

oon we were clattering through Liverpool's streets toward the docks. As we approached, I saw the masts of huge ships reaching to the sky. Beyond was the ocean, shimmering and vast. Could I really do this? I remembered Father's voice chiding me from the stone. "I'm going with her," I whispered and hoped he would be pleased. If he could chide me from a stone, could he also protect me on a ship, wherever he was?

"Yonder's the *Parthenon*," said the driver. He had stopped next to a long dock. The huge ship moored there had the name *Parthenon* paraded across the bow. There was nothing to do but alight from the coach.

"They will be expecting you?" the driver asked.

"Yes," I lied.

The driver handed my trunks to two porters. *They will probably want tips,* I thought. I just hoped they wouldn't run away with my bags. The driver doffed his hat and said, "Pleasant voyage, miss." George had clearly instructed the driver to stay with me, but he closed the carriage door, remounted the box, and soon disappeared into the crowd.

I clutched my parasol as if it were a life preserver and followed the men with my trunks. We walked the length of the dock, and the men began to climb the gangplank to the ship.

As I drew closer, I could hear the ship creak and shift in the water. My head spun. Was I moving or was the ship? I put one hand on a rope and began to climb the wooden walkway. I clung to the rope, certain I would be pitched into the sea at any moment. At the top of the gangplank, the porters waited. For their tips, I assumed. And the face of a crew member looked down at me, not at all pleasantly. I swallowed and looked for Mother. But she was nowhere to be seen.

"Boarding papers, miss?" the crew said.

I swallowed. "I have no papers. My mother is on board. I have come to join her." The porters eyed me incredulously.

"I can't allow you onto the ship without papers," said the crewman. He looked happy to make this announcement.

"Please find my mother, and I'm sure we will get this sorted," I said.

"Sorry," said the crew. "No papers, no entrance. Them's the rules."

All three men were scowling at me now. I wanted to run back to George and Sarah.

"Miss Mima?" said a familiar voice. It was Brother Bradshaw, the Mormon emigration agent. I had nearly forgotten how kind his blue eyes were. His smile was so welcoming that I was suddenly afraid I might cry.

"Good heavens, Jack," Brother Bradshaw said. "Is this any way to welcome a young lady to our ship? Have her items stowed at once." Brother Bradshaw offered me a handkerchief.

Jack glared at me but nodded at two other crew members, who hoisted up my trunks and disappeared. Brother Bradshaw handed a coin to each porter and helped me step onto the vessel. "So, my dear," he said, "you decided to join your mother after all. She will be grateful to see you." I nodded, unsure of whether to trust my voice yet.

Mother stood on the deck of the ship, small and pensive.

"Sister Hough," Brother Bradshaw called to her. "Look who I found wandering the docks."

Mother turned. When she glimpsed me, her face registered pure shock. "Mima!" she said. She enfolded me into her arms and held me as tight as the ship's rigging.

When she let me go, I fondly brushed a tear from her cheek. "You see, Mother," I said, "I will not let those Mormons have you without a fight."

She smiled at me as if my face were the most beautiful sight in the world. Brother Bradshaw chuckled and disappeared. I took her arm, and we strolled across the ship. From the deck, we could see all of Liverpool harbor. When we turned, the water stretched to the horizon. The crew scurried about, carrying ropes and sea tackle.

"I am determined to see you safely to Zion," I continued. "I hope it is as lovely as you seem to believe. But what if the streets aren't truly paved with gold, the buildings topped with diamonds? You need a brave, young daughter to see you safely to such a place. And to remind you to enjoy the journey as well. "

"Mima, whatever would I have done without you?" Mother said. Her voice was light and teasing, yet I knew she meant every word.

I felt for the moment that I had made the right choice. No matter where we were bound, we would be together, as we had ever been. To lose her would be to lose half myself. I had reclaimed a piece of home.

Shortly before supper, all the passengers were called to gather on the main deck of the ship. A tall man in a spotless uniform was introduced as Captain Woodbury. He welcomed us to the ship and explained the rules for cleaning the hold, preparing meals, and handling procedures during storms. As he spoke I looked at the other passengers. There were only twenty of us; the ship was filled mostly with cargo. A father held a young boy on his lap. His wife sat proud and straight, even while she clutched a tiny babe. A man and a boy about my age sat beside them. Two older women sat together, and two other families sat apart, their dress and language immediately identifying them as foreigners, from Scandinavia, perhaps.

Captain Woodbury finished talking about the rules and drew something from his pocket. He held up a turquoise gem, shimmering in the sun. "This is sea glass," he said. "It was first used by ancient Romans and later washed up on the beaches of Cyprus. I carry it to remind myself that you can never underestimate what the ocean is capable of. The sea is both cruel and kind. May God smile upon this journey."

I longed to hold the sea glass and inspect it more closely, but when Captain Woodbury finished speaking, Brother Bradshaw stepped forward. "Brothers and sisters, welcome to the *Parthenon*. This great ship is the vessel that will bear you safely, God willing, to Zion. I am here to organize this company so that order and goodwill may prevail. I have asked William Howell to act as president of the company." A stout, grizzled man stood and swept off his hat.

Brother Bradshaw gave out various assignments for ship duty. He concluded by saying, "Brother James Seymour and I are missionaries, and we are quite anxious to be returning home." He smiled, and his eyes twinkled. "We will hold religious services several times a week, as well as on the Sabbath, of course. All in good health should attend."

I sucked in my breath as I realized for the first time that I was likely the only person on board who was not a Mormon.

Brother Bradshaw asked for a sustaining vote and then dismissed the company. As people left to get settled, he came towards us and took my hand. "I trust the hymnal will be helpful. It is one of the few on board."

"I am sure it will," I said, hoping that he would not press me further.

I looked for Captain Woodbury to inquire about the sea glass, but he had disappeared.

That night Mother and I huddled together in our narrow bunk, uncomfortable on the scratchy straw. I lay awake, unable to sleep, listening to the ceaseless noises of the ship—the cry of a baby, the noise of people tossing in their sleep, the creak of ship timbers, and above all the slapping sound of waves breaking against the side of the boat—pushing us one way, only to send us bobbing back to the other side. I lay awake in the darkness, listening to the creaks and groans, sensing the merciless power that coursed through the waves. When I finally slept, my dreams were splashed with murky, muddy waters.

A tugboat towed us into the channel at dawn. Some passengers cheered and sang. Others prayed. Mother linked her arm through my own. She shed tears, and I was surprised to feel a twinge of anger course through me. Anger because she had made this choice, a choice that had forced my own.

I pulled my arm away and hurried to the top deck, where I watched the green shores of England slowly swim to the edge of the horizon and slip into the sea. All my plans were leaving with it—all expectation of what my life would hold. We were headed into a new life, with little understanding of what awaited us there. The ship surged under me, and I grasped the ship railing to steady myself.

"Will you ever feel at home elsewhere, do you suppose?"

I jumped, startled. The voice was right beside me, when I had thought I was alone. I turned and looked into a woman's eyes—brown, soulful, and fiercely dry. It was the woman with the baby. She still clutched the baby wrapped in blankets, while the wind snatched and tore at the edges. Her husband and little boy were nowhere in sight.

"My home no longer exists," I told her.

"Nor does mine," she said. "It is the lot of the emigrant to be trapped between two lands, never comfortable anywhere. But Elizabeth, now," she shook the blankets gently, "she will never remember the old, and she'll wonder why I cannot love the new." Her face twisted at the irony.

"If you are certain you cannot love your new land, then why make the journey?" I asked.

"Because my husband is going. I'm going with him."

I was intrigued by this woman, whose plight was so similar to my own and yet so different. "You do not wish to join the other Mormons?"

She laughed. "As I'm not a Mormon myself, I have no wish to join them." Shock must have filled my face, because she added, "Do not be alarmed. I am a Methodist."

I recovered my composure and guaranteed her I was not alarmed. "I am surprised to meet another, for I too am not a Mormon. I am traveling with my mother."

She tucked a hand through my arm and smiled. "I am Mary Bennion, and we must be friends. We will be two black-hearted souls in the white city of Zion."

I allowed her to take my hand. I looked for the last glimpse of England; each passing minute more waves surged between us. In spite of Mary's hand upon my own, as I watched the gray waters stretch away from us, like a length of fabric ever unfolding, all I could feel was apprehension.

CHAPTER FIFTEEN

I grew accustomed to the constant rocking of the ship. For the first few days we made our way around by holding onto whatever happened to be close by. But after a few days most of the passengers got their sea legs, although a few of the older ones still complained of headaches from the constant motion.

We passed other ships—a Dutch vessel and an English schooner—all bound for the New World and whatever awaited us there. Porpoises frolicked around the bow, playfully dancing among the waves.

On deck, when the weather was fair, the days were tolerable. I could pretend that I wasn't going to the Mormon Zion, which I learned was a city named Nauvoo. I could pretend I wasn't going anywhere. I was simply suspended in time and space, adrift upon an endless ocean, where both past and future were lost in the distant hazes.

I loved staring out at the sea. It constantly shifted, shimmering with strength, like a tiger lovely in its sleep. I had never known so many shades of blue and green and gray, varying as the sun rolled across the sky. And although I could barely swim, I found myself wanting to dive into the murky depths, to be swallowed up in this great, mighty whole, to be a part of something beautiful and grand. I found secret corners of the ship, where I could lean over the railing as far as possible, bending over the gorgeous, glistening waves, watching the sunlight try to pierce the depths in descending shards of light. I longed to be held in its seamless embrace.

When I stared so long that the water began to fill my head with strange thoughts and I feared that I really might throw myself overboard, I went in search of Mary. I could have made friends with the boy my own age, but Mary drew me like a magnet. I found her fascinating because nothing about her made sense. She did not look like a mother. She was strong and sinewy, beautiful and straight as the mast of the ship. She held her children kindly and yet slightly apart from her. She spoke to her children as if they were adults. Even the baby, who could not even crawl, she addressed with candor. She was incredibly strong, and yet she was following her husband across the sea to an unknown land. She was not a Mormon, yet she was going to live among them. More than anything else, I was intrigued by the sorrow in her eyes. She never spoke of its source, and I would not ask her, but when I looked in her eyes, I remembered Father and Providence House and all that I had lost.

Mary could not have been more different from Charlotte if she had tried. While Charlotte was young and plump and blonde and gay, Mary was older and thin and dark and cynical. But my friendship with Mary began to soothe the raw edges of Charlotte's betrayal. And Mary knew, more than anyone else, what I had been through with Mother joining the Mormons. She had lived through it herself.

Mother watched me with Mary, perhaps envious of our friendship. I felt her eyes upon us, yet I did not know how to bridge the gulf between us. It was the worst irony, for I had left England and all my hopes of Liverpool to be with Mother. And now that I was with her, I could not forgive her for the sacrifice I had made. It was cruel, but I could not stop it any more than I could stop the rushing of the sea.

CHAPTER SIXTEEN

A week into our journey, we had some days of foul weather. Dense fog surrounded us, and when the rains came, the deck was covered with water several inches deep. The ship became a cold, dank, miserable place. Sleeping was nearly impossible, and I could have sworn the ship rolled over several times each night. It was impossible to keep our footing while walking on deck, where we sat for meals, holding our plates firmly to prevent their running away. One night beautiful lightning lit up the whole horizon.

The weather broke after a few agonizing days. Then the sea was covered with foam, and shoals of flying fish played off the bow. I found a corner of the ship, a place I imagined to be mine alone, and drew a sigh of great relief, but I should have known I would not be able to keep the spot to myself forever. Brother Bradshaw found me in my cramped deck corner. He swept off his hat and apologized for interrupting, although I was only staring at the ocean. I had time enough to be grateful that I wasn't leaning over the railing at the moment he appeared.

His eyes were as blue as the waves receding from my view and far kinder. "Good afternoon, Miss Mima. I thought I might find you here."

"Does my mother need me?" I asked.

"Oh, no. Don't trouble yourself." He turned his eyes out to the sea. "A lovely sky, isn't it?" He seemed to be searching the clouds. "I wonder if you are familiar with a certain scripture in Isaiah? It says, 'The redeemed of the Lord shall come with singing unto Zion.'"

"I cannot recall it," I admitted.

"Ah, yes," he said. "Well, of course one cannot know them all." He clasped his hands behind his back, and I wondered what he could possibly be talking about. "Perhaps you would help me with that scripture, Miss Mima?"

I was now completely confused, but he quickly added, "What I mean is, there is little musical talent on board. I know you are not of our faith, but I wonder if you might help our meetings with a song from time to time?"

Now it was my turn to look to the sea. I had not sung since leaving Providence House. I had begun to wonder if I would ever want to sing again. Had my song remained behind, trapped in the house, woven among the sunshine and the cabbage roses? I wanted to sing, my throat ached with the absence of song, and yet . . . I couldn't. I looked back at his kind, waiting eyes. "I cannot sing the songs of a religion I don't believe in," I said at last.

"I understand," he said. He paused. "I only ask that you read through the hymnal. If there are any songs you feel fit your own faith, perhaps you would be willing to share them with us. I would be most grateful."

I looked back at the sea, searching the green-blue-gray for an answer, but certainty was lost in the hues and shadows. I thought of how kind Brother Bradshaw had been—the gift of the hymnal and his help on the day I boarded the ship. His blue eyes sparkled. How could I refuse? "Yes, I will look through the book," I said at last.

His smile repaid me. "Thank you. Good day, Miss Mima," he said, retreating.

When he was gone, I retrieved the small hymnal from my berth and returned to my secret spot, which no longer seemed so secret. I opened the book cautiously but found myself surprised. Certainly there were strange and unfamiliar songs, and because the book did not contain the scores, I did not know how they would sound. There were songs about Joseph Smith's vision of God and songs about the golden bible and the imminent destruction of the world. And even one that talked about Nephites. But there were others, dearly familiar, like old friends—hymns such as "Sweet Is the Work, My God, My King," and "I Know That My Redeemer Lives." As I read the familiar words of these hymns, lullabies from my childhood, I was taken back to the shadowy sweet echoes of St. Peter's and the hours spent in the choir stall with Charlotte at my side, singing the lauds, Vespers, and

Complines. I remembered the man in the psalm, so long ago, as if it were another lifetime, another Mima who had stood in St. Peter's, pitying that man fleeing on a tiny boat to Zion. I felt new kinship with that man. I would have liked to find that psalm and wished my knowledge of scripture were more thorough.

One hymn caught my attention. I had sung it many times but had never taken notice of the words until now. With the endless sea in front of me, they took on new meaning:

> God's wisdom's vast, and knows no bound,
> A deep where all our thoughts are drown'd.

I spoke the line over and over, as I gazed into the rolling sea. Was this mighty sea the repository of God's wisdom? If so, my thoughts were just a piece of driftwood, floating upon the fathomless deep, while God was unfathomable, unknowable, like the sea.

As I pondered the words, the melody played through my head, filling me with the desire for song. It had been too long since I had last sung for the simple joy of it. I held the book away from me, filling my lungs full of sea air, crisp with salt, and facing God's ocean, I sang.

CHAPTER SEVENTEEN

I hadn't realized how much I had missed singing. It felt so good to hold my stomach taut, lifting out a heavy song that lay like a weight upon my heart. I had no desire to stop. I sang every song I knew in the hymnal. As I sang, my heart grew light, filled with the sunshine of home.

And so a week later, I sat next to Mother at the Mormon Sunday service, awaiting my turn to sing. I passed the sacrament bread and cup without partaking and hardly heard the words that were spoken. But when my turn came to sing, my voice lingered upon the notes, stretching them out, for I did not want them to end. As I sang I watched the sea, and I pictured my song being swept up by the waves, washed into the repository of God's knowledge. It was only after I finished that I remembered the audience was even there at all.

When the meeting ended, Brother Bradshaw approached me. The boy my age and a man I took to be his father were with him. Brother Bradshaw said, "Thank you, Miss Mima. Your song was lovely. Have you made the acquaintance of the Farndons?" He indicated the boy and his father.

I shook my head.

"This is Joshua Farndon and his son, Will," said Brother Bradshaw.

I curtseyed.

"Pleased to make your acquaintance, Miss Hough," said Joshua Farndon. "You have a lovely voice."

"Thank you," I said. My eyes lingered upon his son's face. Will Farndon looked to be about sixteen. His brown hair fell in curls, and his eyes were as dark as the sea.

"Will plays the violin," said Brother Farndon, nodding to his son.

"Truly?" I asked.

Will shrugged off his father's praise. "I haven't played recently, but I hope to join the orchestra in Nauvoo," he said.

"Is there an orchestra there?" I asked.

"Oh, yes, and a good one, if the tales are true," said Brother Farndon.

"And a choir?" I asked.

"Of course," he said. "Emma Smith compiled the Church's hymnal."

"She did?" I was shocked. The tales I had heard of Nauvoo never included anything about music. Although I had heard talk of devilish dancing.

"Perhaps Will could play his violin tomorrow evening after supper. It has been put away too long."

Will looked at his father with an expression I could not read. "Perhaps," he said. His eyes flicked back to me. "Will Miss Hough bring her voice as well?"

"Thank you. Perhaps I will."

Nothing could have kept me from it. The afternoon was sluggish with anticipation. Assisting Mother with dinner seemed impossible. Sick of my fussing, she asked, "Mima, you are feeling unwell? You may go lie down if you are ill."

"I feel fine," I admitted sullenly.

She lowered her voice. "Then please refrain from being peevish."

I pursed my lips in reply.

Finally supper was finished, and the sun set across the water. I went to a spot of deck where I could stand undetected, waiting for Will Farndon to appear. I wondered if he would play well. I hoped he would not play poorly. Finally I saw him: a silhouette, with the beautiful shape of the violin black against the sky. I saw him hesitate, looking about the deck in the falling dusk.

"Mr. Farndon," I called, walking towards him.

"Miss Hough," he replied. "I thought you would not come."

"Yet here I am," I said.

"Then let us see if I can recall how to play." He sat down upon a crate and began to tune the strings. Other passengers heard the cheerful plunking and gathered toward us. Will's father stood near the deck railing. Mary and her husband came and stood beside me as Will applied rosin to the bow. Then he began to play.

In my opinion, the violin is the instrument with the greatest potential for good or ill. I can't imagine sharing a house with a new violin student, screeching and shrieking out calamitous notes. But when it is played with mastery, the violin is like liquid sound, flowing out in a steady stream of loveliness. Will Farndon could play. Someone brought a lantern, but I think Will could have played the violin with only the feel of the strings to guide him. The look on his face was pure pleasure.

I don't remember who started the dancing. But it seemed natural. Inevitable. Mother had always frowned upon dancing in England, because Reverend Buckley discouraged it. Mother said that dancing was for peasants. But I had always loved it. My respect for Mormons soared. I soon found that no dance hall on earth can compare with dancing upon the deck of a ship, under the open sky, to the throaty flow of the violin. Brother Bradshaw acted as prompter, and we danced the quadrille, a motley mix of old and young and everyone in between. Age and skill did not matter. All that mattered was the music and the stamp of feet upon the deck. The stars came out, peppering the sky, reflected in the water until the waves were awash with tiny dancing lights.

After several tunes, the dancers began to sit down.

Will paused. "Miss Hough?"

"Yes."

"Would you care to join me?"

I blushed into the darkness at the boldness of his words. "I assume you wish me to sing?"

"I believe you know 'Praise Ye the Lord'?"

I was startled to hear the name of the hymn I had recently been singing. Had my private singing sessions on deck been more public than I had imagined? "I . . . do," I stammered.

He sounded the opening strains of the hymn, and for some reason I felt shaky. My notes began hesitantly, until at last I forgot about everything except the music. I lingered upon the lines that I had pondered earlier, "His wisdom's vast, and knows no bound, / A deep where all our thoughts are drown'd," and wondered again about Will's uncanny choice. I heard my own voice and felt like it belonged to someone else. It seemed richer, fuller, and softer somehow. Perhaps it was the moonlight.

We sang several more songs, and at last people began to drift away. I saw Mary leave, holding her husband's arm, her eyes resting kindly on my face.

"We seem to have lost our audience," I said at last.

"But that is no reason to stop," Will replied. "I could play right through the night. I put my violin away for too long."

"Why have you not played before tonight?" I asked.

"That is a complicated question, Miss Hough." Will paused to consider, idly fingering the violin strings. "Perhaps it was too much tied up with home." He sighed, and sorrow hung in the air between us. "And with people there."

I nodded, hoping he would continue.

But he stood up instead. "Father is right—I had put it away too long. A violin is built for a journey, and I cannot be long without it."

I knew precisely what he meant.

"How did you learn to sing, Miss Hough?"

"I sang with a parish church choir," I replied. "And studied music on the pianoforte. I could not bring it with me," I said, a touch of sadness in my voice.

"I'm sorry you had to leave it behind."

"We all had to leave things behind," I said. "The music lets us forget, but this ship is full of heartache."

"Will the heartache increase or decrease with time, do you suppose?" he asked.

I had no answer for him.

"Miss Hough, I bid you goodnight. It was a pleasure." I curtseyed. His eyes were pained, but I did not think the blame was mine. My eyes returned to the ocean and found the water harsh and dark and cold. I wondered who Will Farndon had left behind. And I cursed the water that, mile by mile, wrenched our lives apart.

CHAPTER EIGHTEEN

*A*t breakfast the next morning, Mary sought me out. She settled herself next to me and leaned in close. "I enjoyed your singing last night, Mima. Music under the moonlight is most heavenly."

"Master Beethoven certainly agrees with you," I said, thinking of his "Moonlight" Sonata.

She refused to be diverted. "And with such accompaniment. Truly you and Mr. Farndon are quite an accomplished duo." She smiled, her eyes innocent and wide.

I would not have thought Mary capable of pressing for confidence. She had her own secrets to hide. "Yes, he is quite a musician," I agreed.

"And close to your own age, isn't he?"

"I believe so. And quite Mormon, as well," I replied.

"Mormons occasionally marry outside the faith," Mary responded at once.

"Not if their mothers can help it," I said.

Mary laughed. "Oh, Mima. There is little romance in your heart."

"None at all," I replied.

"But consider his violin," she said.

"He does play divinely, I'll give you that. But I think he left his heart in England. He spoke of it last night. "

"You cannot leave your heart across the ocean when you're only sixteen."

"I'm not so sure," I responded. "Mary, isn't it curious that we spend so much time together but know nothing at all about the lives we lived before this journey? I'm sure there are many secrets on board."

"Not all secrets are worth discovering," Mary said, and I was surprised at how quickly her voice had become bitter.

I pressed my friend's hand. I did love her, in spite of her hidden sorrow. Perhaps because of it. "And what if you fling a secret into the ocean?" I asked. "Do you think it will be swallowed by a fish? Or wash up on a distant beach in Cyprus? Come, I have one to be rid of. Will you join me?" I tugged on her hand.

"I have changed my mind about your romantic condition, Mima," Mary said with a laugh.

I pulled her to the rail. I whispered a secret into my hand and then flung it far onto the silky waves. Mary followed suit.

"You see?" I said. "It is like the song says: 'A deep where all our thoughts are drowned.' God has swallowed up our secrets."

"If only they could stay there forever," Mary said.

"Oh, the ocean will hold them. Until we are ready to have them back. I imagine it is like the sea glass Captain Woodbury spoke of. Ancient Romans tossed sharp, cruel glass into the ocean, and it came back smooth and lovely. Your secret goes in painful and sharp, but it will come back to you washed and rounded, made soft by the sea."

Mary smiled. "It is a lovely hope, Mima. Thank you."

That night I awoke in my berth, tossed awake by a wretched dream of home: Providence House lit up with flames. The fire had been so bright and glaring, I was shocked to open my eyes in blackness. For a moment I waited, expecting to hear the silence of home. But instead there were the dreadful noises of the ship—creaking, groaning, and the endless washing of waves. The blankets were damp and twisted about me, like a rope. I flung them off and lay panting in the darkness. The air was hot and oppressive. I groped through my trunk, found my dressing gown, and flung it over my shoulders. Mother's breathing was deep and steady. I crept from our berth.

Climbing the ladder in the darkness, I stepped onto the main deck. It felt like a sin to be out at night by myself. Remembering moonlit walks home from Evensong, I reminded myself that I did not need a chaperone. I never had. The night air was cold and bracing. The sky was a thick blanket of stars, and a waning moon floated on the water. I found a corner where I could face the ocean and listen to the lapping of the waves against the ship. I filled my lungs with the night air, moist and salty but fabulously fresh. The ship rolled beneath me, like a great wooden cradle. The terror of the dream began to ebb.

Across the ship, so faintly I wondered if I were imagining it, came the sound of music. A few strains, and then nothing. I strained toward the sound. Had I imagined it? It came again. Clear and languorous, rising above the noise of the ship. Faint but growing stronger. The melody seemed to arise from the night itself. I listened, trying to make out the tune. The notes of the violin rose and fell and rose again, and as they sounded, my heart filled with intense emotion. That song—what was it?

I did not know it by name, but I could not escape the feeling that I had heard it before. My chest heaved. The notes continued, heartbreaking, beautiful and clear—so beautiful they pained me, so exquisite I wanted them to stop, and yet I wanted them never to stop. The notes rose to a sustained pitch—one piercingly clear, resonant note. What was this song? How did I know it? For I could have finished it, although I had no words to match it, my mind knew the last notes before they were played. The last phrase resolved, hung in the air for a moment, and then was gone. Only the sound of the waves splashing against the ship remained, falling with a gentle shushing noise, as if to calm me.

Where had I heard the song before? Could such a song have a composer? It seemed to me it must have sprung, fully formed, from an aching heart—pure longing turned into sound. It was as if Will (for it must have been Will) had been playing a love song to home.

I eventually made my way back to my berth, but the melody played over and over in my mind, chasing sleep far away.

CHAPTER NINETEEN

he next morning, Mother reached for my hand as I tried to flee
to the deck.

"Help me with my lace class, Mima," she said.

"All I know about lace is from you, Mother. How could I possibly
help?"

"I need another pair of skilled hands," she said. "Please come."

I sighed. An hour later I sat on the deck, part of one of the classes
I had tried to avoid. "One, two, three, four loops: cow hitch, two, three,
four half-hitch knots; then double stitch around the core thread and
back again." Mother's voice carried across the deck of the ship, and if
it had not been for the constant rocking of the ship, I might have supposed myself back at Providence House with a tatting shuttle. But the

sun beat down upon the rough wooden planks of the deck where most of the women had gathered to learn the skill of lace making.

At least Mary sat beside me with her son John, who was five years of age. She held the shuttle on her lap and moved her fingers in labored movements. She moved her hands slowly but with resolve, and the lace would be fine. Ruth Teal, the elderly woman, leaned close to her lace work, but she continually knotted the thread. Mother walked among us, stopping here to nod encouragement, there to straighten a loop. When she got to Ruth, she sat down beside her. "Here, Sister Ruth, let me help you with these knots." Ingar Jensen and Agnes Forsgren sat together, working fine stitches, speaking in Swedish.

I was far more interested in Mary's son John than in the lace. He was a mischievous little fellow with brown snapping eyes and sandy hair.

"Here, John," I entreated him to my knee. "What do you plan to do when you get to Joseph's city?"

"I'm going to ride a camel first thing, Miss Mima."

"A camel?" I suppressed a giggle.

"A wild camel. But first I'll have to capture it." Two gangly arms leaned against my knee as he explained how to capture a wild camel. I smiled and listened to his prattle. "I must use sturdy rope," John continued.

Mary leaned toward us. "John, are you tiring Miss Mima's ears?"

I smiled at my friend. "Not at all. I enjoy hearing John's plans."

The boat rocked, and Mother asked for attention as she explained a more complicated chain. I leaned forward to watch her explanation, for it was a stitch I had not done for a while. Suddenly I realized the little elbows were removed from my lap and nowhere in sight. "Mary," I said, "where is John?"

Her eyes snapped up from the lace she was working and darted across the deck. My own eyes followed hers, but I could not find the small, sandy head. Mary threw the lace to the floor and crossed the ship. I walked after her.

She searched the deck and then turned towards the hold.

"Perhaps he is with Samuel," I said. Mary descended the ladder and ran to her berth.

"Samuel," she called.

"Yes."

"Is John with you?"

"I thought he was on deck. I have not seen the lad."

Mary collapsed in hysterics. Samuel held her, unsure what to do.

"Go!" said Mary, still sobbing.

Samuel let go of her and rushed to the deck.

I stood still, feeling intensely useless. "The boy could be anywhere," I said to Mary.

"Go search," she said between sobs. I left her on the floor and fled to the deck. All the other passengers were helping now.

I stopped by the railing and looked at the waves. John was curious. He was a strong climber and easily might do something silly, like climb over a railing to have a better look at the sea below. Steely waves stretched in every direction, capable of swallowing the entire ship without a ripple. I shuddered and turned away. If he was there, we would never find him.

Mother and Sister Jensen began searching the main deck's barrels and crates, while Ruth tied her knotted strings into a bundle.

By this time Samuel and a few other men were searching through sails and coils of rope. I realized how enormous this ship was and how many places there were to hide a tiny boy.

I wondered if I should alert Captain Woodbury. I hastened to his cabin and peered through the open port window into his quarters. There sat John, quite comfortable on the captain's lap, dipping a sugar lump into the man's coffee.

"Brother Bennion!" I called. He heard the urgency in my voice and rushed across the deck toward me. I pointed into the captain's quarters. He looked at his little boy sitting on the captain's lap, and the tension drained from his face.

He knocked on the door and entered without waiting for an invitation. "I'm very sorry, sir, but we must get this boy to his mother," Samuel told the captain.

"We were talking about camels," John said, with a pout.

Samuel lifted John into a tight embrace, and I followed as he carried the boy back to Mary. She lay on the floor of the hold, exactly where I had left her, still sobbing and crying. She sat up as Samuel placed John in her arms, but she continued to cry, rocking him, kissing him, sobbing and sobbing. I clung to the shadows, watching my friend, struggling to understand her hysteria. Her boy was safe. He was returned, but still she sobbed.

"I could not lose you," she said. "I could not lose you, too." And finally I realized that it was not John for whom she cried.

CHAPTER TWENTY

*F*or the rest of the journey, Mary refused to let the boy out of her sight. Only when he lay asleep in the berth did she leave him to pace the deck, staring out at the sea. I longed to talk to her, but I did not know how to begin. I understood her secret only slightly more than I had before. I had always felt close to her, but her worry as a mother was something I couldn't relate to. Her children were wry, funny creatures, and it seemed to me that if I were their mother, I would want to spend more time playing with them than worrying about them.

I soon grew weary of our journey. I helped Mother with classes. I cooked our meals. I cleaned our sleeping area. I sang, sometimes alone and sometimes accompanied by Will Farndon. Although I had no longing to see the Mormons' Zion, my feet were ready to find firm ground, and my stomach was ready for something to eat besides sour potatoes, boiled beans, rancid water, and dried biscuits.

As we neared the tropics, the sunrises became streaked with fire. Orange visions of clouds painted streaking trails across the sky. The water reflected the view until it seemed the whole sea would be consumed by the flame. On the third morning of the sun's display, I stood close to Captain Woodbury as we marveled at the view. "'Tis a sailor's warning, I'm afraid," he said.

"Sir?"

"A lovely sunrise at sea often heralds a storm, Miss Mima."

Fear stirred within me. So far we had been lucky not to encounter anything worse than a small swell. "I suppose the oceans need storms to form your sea glass?" I asked.

He drew a piece from his pocket and passed it to me. I held it up so it shimmered in the setting sun. "Of a surety, Miss Mima."

"I'm not sure if I'd like to be here to witness waves big enough to turn glass into a gem," I confessed.

He glanced at my face. "We will soon enter the islands, where the seas are calm. Perhaps we will pass in time."

But the next morning, the wind freshened to a gale. The sea was dotted with whitecaps, and the sky grew darker with each passing hour. Mother and most of the other passengers went below, but I refused. I held onto the railing as the crew rushed about the ship, preparing the sails and securing bolt ropes. The sea became an immense cauldron covered with foam, as it began to heave itself into mighty swells that nearly reached the deck of the ship. When the rain came, it flew like gunshot, leaving red welts upon my face and hands. The sound was like a mighty roaring, and conversation became impossible. The ship's bell rang out, ordering all passengers below, and reluctantly I obeyed. The hold was lashed behind us as we descended into blackness. All lanterns had been extinguished for fear of fire.

The smell was horrible—vomit and sweat and chamber pots. But the sounds were awful too: the cries of terrified children, the moans and retching of the seasick. I found our bunk and threw myself upon it, stuffing my hands into my ears, hoping to stop the terrible noises. The ship surged. It seemed to roll from one end to the other, just in time to be tossed back again. Timbers groaned, and I feared we would be smashed into a pile of splinters. At last I grew sick as well, from motion or the stench or both. Mother held my hair as I retched into a chamber pot and then pressed my face into our moldy mattress and wished to die.

A man's hand was laid upon my own, and above the howling of the storm, I heard Brother Bradshaw's voice.

"Sister Hough," he said. He had mistaken me for my mother, but I wasn't about to correct him. "The captain fears there are rocks ahead. We must pray that the Lord will preserve us." The hand withdrew and moved on to the next berth.

Mother took my hands and knelt on the bunk. I thought perhaps we could have stayed lying down for this prayer, but imagining the rocks, I decided to take no chances. Holding onto the bunk for support, I pushed myself onto my knees and somehow clasped my hands together.

"Oh, God," Mother began, "please keep Thy eyes upon us. Protect us as we cross this mighty ocean. Hold us safe within Thy hands . . ."

Her words continued, and I realized that around us in the darkness everyone was praying. The moans and the crying subsided as all the passengers begged God for protection.

" . . . guide us safely through Thy ocean that we may serve Thee in Zion," Mother continued.

Her words were lovely, but all I could think was, "Please don't let us die, Lord. Please don't let us die." I whispered this over and over again into the darkness.

The next moment an enormous cracking sound echoed through the ship. The noise shivered through the boat timbers and shook our berth. Was the ship breaking apart? I screamed and clutched at Mother, waiting for the icy waves to swallow us up.

But they did not come, and the motion of the boat continued as before. For hours we waited, clinging to each other, wondering what had happened. Sometimes Mother prayed. Sometimes she sang to me. Her voice made it better and worse at the same time. It comforted me, and yet it reminded me of home, which had never seemed so far away.

Finally, Brother Bradshaw's voice was back. "It is all right. The worst danger has passed. We have come through the storm, praise the Lord."

I was so ill I could hardly move. But I raised my hand and found his sleeve. "Brother Bradshaw?" I asked. "What was that horrible sound? I thought we had run aground on the rocks."

"That sound, Miss Mima, was the Lord's answer to our prayer. It was a crack of lightning, just one. By its light the captain was able to see the rocks through the dark of the storm and bring us to safety."

I lay back upon the bunk, my mind swirling. A crack of lightning. Just one. To guide our ship away from the rocks. Light in the midst of darkness, safety in the midst of a storm. Had it really been a miracle? Did God listen to the Mormon prayers?

"Thank You," I whispered, exhaling into the rancid darkness. Perhaps God wanted us in Zion after all.

CHAPTER TWENTY-ONE

When I awoke, the hold was in chaos. Belongings had been tossed about the ship like confetti, and most of the passengers were still too seasick to leave their beds. Esther Bennett, one of the elderly women, had fallen during the storm and bruised her knee badly. I knew I should help Mother tidy our belongings, but the feeling of claustrophobia was too much.

I fled from the hold and burst into the clear morning sunshine. I could not fill my lungs with enough fresh air. The sea was still dotted with foam but was so calm by comparison it seemed impossible such a storm had ever occurred. Yet rubbish littered the deck, and lines were tangled. The crew scurried about, cleaning and repairing. We spent most of the day scrubbing down the putrid hold.

By the next day, the air had changed in the night, becoming moist and heavy with heat. The water had changed, too. The impenetrable water of the Atlantic had turned to aquamarine. The water was so clear, I could see white slippery shapes of fish pass under the boat. There were no hiding places in this green, glassy ocean. We had passed into the tropics.

At midday the call rang out from the forecastle deck. "Land!"

The captain came and stood beside me at the ship's rail.

"The island of Guadeloupe," said Captain Woodbury, nodding towards a green smudge in the distance.

When we drew closer, lush greenery and mountains stretched to the clouds. Large flocks of seabirds flew overhead. The captain said that the darker patches of water were forests of corals. I marveled at the change in the water. Where had the unfathomable gray water gone? What invisible boundary held the steely Atlantic separate from the translucent Caribbean Sea?

The captain spoke of places with names that felt exotic upon my tongue: Santo Domingo, Cape Tiburon, and Jamaica.

"May I see your piece of sea glass?" I asked.

He offered it to me, and I passed it between my palms. It was the same color as the water, smooth and silky—frosted over with the foam of waves and the pounding of the surf. So much I had learned of the ocean on this journey: it could be both harsh and kind, mighty and gentle. I ran my finger over the gem and felt I held the ocean in the palm of my hand.

"And how did you survive the storm, Miss Mima?" the captain asked. "Unscathed?"

I nodded. "Yes, but humbled," I replied. "I'm sorry, but I've no strong desire to spend my life at sea."

He chuckled and rubbed a hand over his grizzled beard. "Yes, you're not the first to feel that way. Yet like that glass, you are strong. You will survive."

"In spite of oceans and Mormons and mothers," I said.

He smiled.

"Thank you," I said, handing the sea glass back to him.

That evening we dropped anchor at one of the islands to take on fresh water and supplies. A small boat pulled alongside us, selling oysters. Mother and I bought a few pounds and made a delicious stew for dinner. I could not drink enough fresh water.

But two days later, I found myself reconsidering the captain's words about survival. The winds dropped, and the sails hung slack. We were becalmed—a common enough occurrence, I was told. To stand still upon the sea, water lapping at the ship under a drooping parasol of sails, was more than I could stand. I grew numb with frustration and paced the length of the deck, cursing the nonexistent wind.

Will Farndon, also on deck, sensed my frustration. "Ships are often becalmed for days and even weeks in the tropics. Do you plan to pace the whole time, Miss Mima?"

"If necessary, Mr. Farndon." I tossed him a grimace and moved to the upper deck, where I resumed my pacing in peace.

Although I had no strong desire to reach Joseph's city, I did not want to remain forever adrift upon this aqua sea, beautiful though it was. Without a breeze, the heat was oppressive. I longed to throw myself into the cooling waves. Just when I thought I surely must go mad with the frustration, Will Farndon reappeared, violin in hand.

"Afternoon, Miss Hough. I thought perhaps you would like some music to accompany your pacing." A smile played about his eyes.

"I'm told that ships are often becalmed for days and weeks at a time, Mr. Farndon," I replied. "Do you plan to play the whole time?"

He laughed. "If necessary, Miss Hough. The time would pass more easily with music than with pacing, methinks."

I surveyed his face, his eyebrows raised jauntily, and smiled at last in spite of myself. "Very well, then."

He played a lively tune, and although it was much too warm for dancing, I felt the anxiety ebb from me, replaced with his song.

After a time, he lowered his bow, and we sat in easy silence. "It appears you are no longer pacing," he said at last.

"When you appeared, I was ready to throw myself overboard in frustration," I replied.

"The music helped, Miss Hough?" He smiled. He did have a beautiful smile. A smile that played around his eyes as well as his mouth. And eyes the color of coffee.

"Oh, yes," I said.

"Well, then, I have repaid a favor," he said.

"I don't believe you owed me a favor," I said.

"Perhaps not one that you knew of."

"I'm happy to have helped."

He glanced at me, trying to decide if he should say more. I did my best to look trustworthy. "Do you remember your song at service?" he asked.

I nodded.

"I told you that I had not played my violin since I left home. But I did not tell you that each day I did not play, it became more difficult to return to. And eventually I feared I would never play again." He paused and glanced at me again. "But when I heard your song, my fingers could not be still."

"A gift of music repaid with a song," I said. He smiled again, and I found myself wishing he would not stop.

At last I dared to ask him the question that had plagued me. "Mr. Farndon, several nights ago I happened to be up on deck. You were playing a song I had not heard you play before."

He nodded.

"What was the name of the song?" I asked.

"Sing the melody," he said.

I hummed the opening phrase for him.

Will picked up his bow, placed the violin on his shoulder, and joined seamlessly onto the note I was singing. The song surrounded me, incredibly familiar, yet impossibly remote. How did I know this song? Longing washed over me, just as before. The notes caught in my chest, and my breathing became ragged. I turned so Will would not see.

He played to the end of the piece and waited while the music seeped into the ship and the sea.

Finally I trusted my voice enough to ask, "Does the song have words?"

He glanced at me curiously. "It is called 'The Water Is Wide,'" he said.

I nodded. Somewhere from the misty shadows of memory, the phrase returned to me: *The water is wide, I cannot cross o'er.* But I could not say how I knew the phrase nor why it seemed to cause my heart to vibrate like a bell.

"Thank you, Mr. Farndon," I said after several long moments had passed. "It is a lovely song."

His eyes were filled with questions, but he only nodded.

CHAPTER TWENTY-TWO

The next morning a breeze began to stir, and at last wind puffed out the canvas sails. We were underway again. I heaved an enormous sigh of relief as the ship cut through the glassy water. After several days of sailing through the tropics, I saw the water change once more. The crystalline water turned muddy and brown. It was river water, and I knew we had reached America at last. I imagined secrets swirling beneath the surface of the waves: Mary's lost baby, the girl who held Will's heart, Mother's reasons for leaving home, and secret hopes of my own, hopes I could not utter because I did not fully know them. Secret shards of glass, waiting to be turned into gems by the sand and waves.

At the bar, a steamboat drew alongside and pulled us up the Mississippi River. The river was so wide that four large ships could easily sail side by side. Our first glimpse of America was rather discouraging. Muddy swamps and rushes stretched out on all sides. But after we had traveled on the river for most of the morning, plantations came into view. The houses were built with verandas on every side, many with honeysuckle and jessamine growing all around. We glimpsed houses built on poles and Negroes plowing fields with teams of oxen. A heavenly fragrance wafted toward us from groves of peach and plum trees in blossom. Wild geese and storks flew overhead. Soon we could see factories and riverboats and came at last to the thriving levee of New Orleans. As at Liverpool, the docks swarmed with people and packages being loaded and unloaded.

As we bade Captain Woodbury good-bye, he pressed a piece of the sea glass into my hand. "Good-bye, Miss Hough. I have enjoyed our conversations on deck and wish you a pleasant journey."

"Thank you," I said, greatly surprised. I rushed after Mother, holding my tiny treasure in my skirts. As soon as they placed the walkways, I rushed to firm ground, only afterwards looking back for Mother and our parcels. The ground felt solid and secure and so heavenly I wanted to fall upon it. I saw Will watching me, laughing.

Mother joined me at last, and we walked along the dock. I noticed people pointing in our direction, whispering with unkind stares. One man said, "Are you headed to Nauvoo? You'd best stay here, miss. I hear they have plenty of trouble in the city of Zion."

Brother Bradshaw took my elbow and led me through the crowd. "The sooner we leave this city of Babylon the better," he said. "Ripening in iniquity."

Fear prickled up my spine. What did the man mean?

"Don't get too attached to the terra firma, Miss Mima," said Brother Bradshaw. "We're transferring to the first riverboat heading north."

Sure enough, our belongings were soon stowed, and we were underway. Black smoke belched from the boat, and an enormous paddle ploughed the water. I stood with Mother by the railing, watching New Orleans slip away. Although some of the buildings in the city were stone, most were made of wood, hammered together hastily. Compared with the stone and brick of England's buildings, the town seemed flimsy. It looked like the whole city might blow away with one good storm.

After several days on the riverboat, we passed the town of St. Louis. It was a bustling hamlet with a lovely riverfront. I thought St. Louis looked pleasant enough, in spite of Brother Bradshaw's description of the city as a den of iniquity. But it disappeared down the river, and we drew close to Nauvoo. My heart was filled with apprehension. We had come so far to find this place. What would await us there?

Brother Bradshaw spoke of it as a perpetual garden of bliss—where people worked and played together in peace and prosperity under the shadow of the glistening temple walls.

But the man in New Orleans said there was trouble in Nauvoo. Which description was correct?

I could not imagine.

Part Two

NAUVOO, ILLINOIS,
UNITED STATES OF
AMERICA

MAY 1845

CHAPTER TWENTY-THREE

here she is," said Brother Bradshaw. "The City of Joseph."

The great Mississippi River continued around a bend, and in the middle of the bend, cradled by the water, was Nauvoo. It was a good-sized town, with a strange conglomeration of buildings—some brick, some frame, and some log cabins. But above all of them was the temple. The building sat high on a bluff with brilliant white walls that seemed to jut into the stainless blue sky. The roof was unfinished. The scene was beautiful but eerie in a way. A building like the temple belonged in a city like Liverpool, but this edifice arose from a scrawny little frontier town. What fanaticism did it represent?

Mother closed her eyes gratefully. "It is so beautiful," she said.

"And to think we will be here to see it finished. It seems unfair that the Prophet did not live to see it."

"How did he die?" I asked.

Brother Bradshaw turned, surprised by the question. "You have not heard the story?"

I shook my head.

He lowered his voice. "The Prophet was taken with his brother to Carthage Jail on false charges. A mob of men with their faces painted black stormed the jail in the middle of the afternoon. They shot Joseph and Hyrum—murdered them in cold blood."

A chill crept through me. Murdered. In the middle of the afternoon. I remembered the man in New Orleans and his warning about trouble in Nauvoo.

"Brother Bradshaw, we are quite safe in this city, aren't we?"

"Well, yes, Miss Mima. Things are quiet now. The Prophet had many enemies, but they're mostly satisfied now that he is gone. We lost the city charter, but you're quite safe here."

"The city charter?" I asked.

"Yes, it was revoked and the militia disbanded."

"But if the militia is disbanded, who will protect the citizens if the mobs return?"

"Our enemies wanted Brother Joseph. And the men will take turns keeping order until the charter is restored. Don't you worry." He tried to smile and then closed his mouth abruptly, as if he had realized that perhaps he shouldn't be discussing this with me. I could not shake off the fear. Why had I not heard about Joseph Smith's murder before?

"Please, sir," I said, "what has happened to Joseph's and Hyrum's families?"

"They are here in Nauvoo, of course." Then he was called from across the boat by another passenger. With a firm nod of his head, he was gone.

I looked at Mother a few feet away, wondering how much of this she knew. "Surely this cannot be Zion," I whispered.

A small group stood on the docks, waving in welcome as we approached. They laid a walkway, and a thickset man came forward and shook hands with many of the passengers. "Welcome to Nauvoo," he said.

Brother Bradshaw stepped forward. "Brother Richards," he said, "how nice of you to welcome us."

"Willard Richards is an apostle," Mother whispered.

An apostle? I wondered. *Like in the Bible?* I looked at the man, who seemed quite ordinary with a dark brown mustache and wool suit. But his eyes were kind, and he seemed sincere as he greeted us.

First to leave the boat were Brother Bradshaw and Brother Seymour, who rushed to embrace their wives and catch up their children, exclaiming over their growth, and holding them as if they would never let go. "They have been away on missions for several years," Mother explained.

I made my escape soon thereafter, resolving to stay on solid ground for as long as possible. Once all the passengers were unloaded, we were gathered together and asked about housing arrangements. The

Forsgrens and Jensens were met by relatives already living in Nauvoo. Mary and Samuel were also met by relatives.

"We have decided to buy a farm at the Mound," Mary explained. "It is five miles away. There are many others from England there. Do come with us."

I looked to Mother. "Oh, thank you, Sister Mary," Mother said, "but Mima and I must stay in town to be close to the sewing guild." I sighed, thinking of all the days of stitching ahead.

"Then you must come and visit," Mary said as she hugged me good-bye.

"I will," I promised. I kissed little John and Elizabeth and curtseyed to Samuel.

Will Farndon and his father were also settling at the Mound. Will bade me good-bye with a tip of his hat. "If you find yourself in need of a song, I am at your service, Miss Mima," he said.

"Thank you, Mr. Farndon," I replied.

Brother Richards turned to Mother. "Have you family here, Sister Hough?"

"I have not," said Mother.

"Are you married?"

"Widowed," she replied.

"There is a row of brick apartments on Kimball Street that may interest you. It is known as Widow's Row, and they are quite affordable."

Mother held her head high. "Thank you, but my daughter and I are self-supporting seamstresses. Do you know of a small house for lease, perhaps near the sewing guild?"

Brother Richards looked surprised. "Why, yes, I believe there is a small home for rent on Parley Street. It belongs to a Brother Cole. Would you like to see it?"

"That would be perfect," said Mother.

As we drove through the town, I peered out the windows at the city I had heard so much about. It really didn't seem so different from the other frontier towns we had passed. The streets were wide and laid out in a grid. They were muddy from spring rains, but here and there flowers were blooming. The town seemed industrious, and there were many houses and other buildings under construction.

By late afternoon we were moving our things into the small home on Parley Street. It was a snug frame home, and although I would have preferred brick, it had a few windows and a small, charming garden. Compared to Providence House, the home seemed like a hovel; yet compared to our quarters on the ship, it felt incredibly spacious.

Next door was a fine brick home, and across the street was a whitewashed log cabin. "Nauvoo is still growing into its own," Brother Cole explained, "so its streets are filling with buildings of all sorts as it slowly becomes a city. They will place the capstone on the temple tomorrow."

"Truly?" said Mother. "What a blessing to be here!"

"You'll have to get up bright and early to make it, ma'am," said Brother Cole with a grin. "Six A.M. to avoid any trouble."

Brother Cole introduced us to our neighbors who were Americans from New York, on one side, and from Ohio, on the other. I could not accustom myself to their manner of speaking. It sounded harsh and flat to me, with no small unkindness done to the vowels.

When Brother Cole departed, Mother looked out at the flower beds in the garden. "Mima, now we can plant the clippings you brought from Providence House."

I looked at the small garden dubiously, remembering the cabbage roses. "There?" I said.

Mother took my hands in hers. "We are home now, daughter. We will stay here. In Zion."

But my heart was not home. And I did not wish to plant the flowers.

Very early the next morning we gathered at the temple to watch as the capstone was laid on top of the white tower. Mary and Samuel were there, and I embraced my friend as if we had been parted for weeks instead of hours.

"What do you think of Zion, Mima?" Mary asked.

I tossed my head. "I must admit I always pictured Zion as a place with fewer bugs."

Mary tittered. "Perhaps the mosquitoes aren't aware this is such a city."

"I think Brigham Young should tell them," I replied.

Mary's eyes danced. "Speaking of which," she said, just as Brother Richards called for everyone's attention.

"Shhh," said Mother, glancing at Mary and me.

Brother Richards welcomed us to the capstone ceremony and introduced Brigham Young. The stone was placed, and the mortar applied. Brigham Young himself pronounced the capstone set and addressed the crowd. He was an imposing man with a booming voice and scratchy-looking beard. He spoke about the temple and the sacrifices that had made it possible. He also spoke of the work that remained to finish the roof and interior and expressed the hope that it would be completed by next spring.

He finished by saying, "The last stone is now laid upon the temple, and I pray the Almighty in the name of Jesus to defend us in this place and sustain us until the temple is finished."

A prickle of fear danced up my back. Would we really need defending?

William Pitt led the Nauvoo Brass Band in a song called "The Capstone March" while I pondered Brother Brigham's words. I held onto Mary's arm and relaxed only when the choir began to sing. It was a well-formed choir. Their sound was full and rich. I wondered if they would allow me, an unbeliever, to sing with them. The ceremony finished with shouts of "Hosannah."

After the ceremony, Mary took my arm. "Come," she said. "I have a surprise for you." She whispered something to Samuel, I waved to Mother, and we moved away from the crowd. Mary directed me up the street from the temple.

"Where are you taking me?"

"You will see," she replied.

She pulled me, laughing, across the street until she stopped abruptly in front of a lovely, single-story brick building. "Here is your surprise," she said.

I read the sign: Nauvoo Music Hall: 1845. "Oh, Mary," I cried. "How did you find it?"

"Samuel's family showed us the town yesterday," she explained. "I knew I had to bring you."

Hope revived in my heart, like a bird flapping its wings. Perhaps I did not have to choose between my past and my future. Perhaps we would be safe here. Perhaps . . . but then I remembered. "Do you suppose they will allow me to sing? A nonbeliever?"

"When they hear your voice, how could they refuse?"

"Mary, you are a dear. Thank you."

CHAPTER TWENTY-FOUR

A month later I stood in the shadows inside the Music Hall, waiting for the curtain to open. The sounds of the audience came from the other side of the curtain—the scuffle of feet, the whisper of paper, and the swish of fabric.

Then the audience grew quiet. Brother Samison, our ancient choir director, must have stepped onto the stage. He spoke in introduction, and the curtains drew open. Brother Samison stepped to the podium and raised his baton in the air.

Forty pairs of eyes focused on his, silently waiting, poised to take flight. The music began, and he drew us in with his hands. He was a marvelous conductor, and I followed his every nuance. Beginning, breathing, singing, placing consonants, drawing out vowels, building here, fading there, rising and falling with his hands.

Sister Hill stood forward from the choir. My concentration shattered. The soloist. I had auditioned for the honor but had been disappointed. Now I would hear the one who had been chosen in my place.

She began, a new hymn finished recently by Sister Eliza R. Snow, a Nauvoo poetess. "How Great the Wisdom and the Love," it was called. The melody soared, the beauty of the song caught in my throat, and I longed to sing it.

But her notes were not well formed. They trembled, occasionally slipping on their way to the true note. And her breath was awkward and choppy.

When she finished, the applause of the audience was energetic. More for the song than for the singer, perhaps? How could she have been chosen?

At the audition Brother Samison had described my voice as promising and brilliant. Why would he have asked for Sister Hill?

It was the choir's turn to sing again, and I pushed these thoughts away, concentrating once more on the music.

When we were finished, I looked up and realized that the lantern above my own head had never been lit. I had remained in the shadow for the entire concert.

"Marvelous," Mother said when it was over.

"Exquisite," said Mary.

"That new song, Mima," Mother said. "Is it not lovely?"

"Sister Eliza has a true genius for poetry," I agreed. "But I am unconvinced that Sister Hill fully displayed it."

Mary and Mother exchanged glances of significance. "Did you hear Brother Samison's introduction?" asked Mother at last.

"I could not hear it through the curtain," I admitted. "Did he speak of the piece?"

"Yes," said Mary, "but do not concern yourself. It matters not."

"Tell me what he said."

"He honored the composer," said Mother. "Of course."

"But what of Sister Hill? Did he speak of her?"

Mary leaned close to me, her hand soft on my arm, her lips warm on my ear. "He said she sang with conviction."

Conviction. Little talent but conviction, which an unbeliever such as myself could never understand. Is that what he had meant? My joy at the concert, the rush of excitement performance brings, shrank within me.

Mary hugged me, offering comfort. I continued to smile and nod and talk, but it was hollow, the joy of it gone. I wanted only to return to the shadows and weep out my fear, fear that I had traded my future for—what? For Mother. She watched me closely, but I turned away into the crowd. Mothers weren't supposed to sacrifice their daughter's dreams for a fanatic religion. The bitterness of regret burned my throat.

CHAPTER TWENTY-FIVE

*W*e made dresses, lace, and corsets to sell at Abel Lamb's consignment store. The store was on Mulholland Street, not far from the temple, and there Brother Abel sold anything that was made in Nauvoo. Bonnets, stockings, and gloves sat alongside our lace. Boots and shoes were displayed on shelves. Chairs, hoes, and pitchforks were in barrels along the wall. People paid Brother Abel with beef, butter, eggs, corn, potatoes, cheese, and fowls. He in turn gave us credit to use in the store. Currency was precious scarce in town, but we did not go hungry. The only pay Mother refused was corn."

"Corn is an Indian food," Sister Beth Ann next door explained. "We make a delicious cake from it."

The next day she brought us some corn bread. Mother and I

thanked her, tasted it, and exchanged glances of surprise. *The texture is not unlike dirt,* I thought. "Don't mention it to Sister Beth Ann," Mother said as I tossed the cake to the chickens.

The long days of stitching were even worse than I had feared. We sewed in the top room of the house, which also served as our bedroom. The space was cramped and wickedly hot. I had always found sewing to be tiresome; now it made me cross. Sewing in a small, cramped room for hours only made me think of Providence House with its cool stone walls and the lifetime that had passed since we last sewed in Mother's store.

One day in August, the heat and humidity became unbearable. Mother and I had an order of corsets to finish, but I flung the needle away and breathed out exasperation.

"Mima," Mother chided, picking my needle up off the floor. "Have you forgotten how dear needles are? We haven't money to throw on the ground."

"Sorry, Mother, but it is much too hot to sew today." Sweat drenched my bodice, and my fingers were cramped and tight from the needle.

"Very well. I will finish the corsets."

"Why would anyone want to wear a corset in this heat? I will help you finish the order, but perhaps tomorrow in the cooler morning hours? I cannot sit here any longer."

"Shall we have tea in the garden?" Mother asked.

"No, I shall ride to Mary's house. It is cooler there."

"Very well." Mother began packing the sewing parcels. I knew she probably wanted me to invite her to the Mound. But truthfully I did not wish for her company.

"I'll be home for supper." I tried to fill my voice with kindness, to ease my guilt.

I had fetched my hat and riding shoes before Mother could say "Very well" a third time.

I borrowed Sister Beth Ann's horse and rode the five miles to the Mound. The wind dried the sweat, cooling my skin. The rush of the wind felt glorious after long hours with the needle. As I rode I pretended I was riding home. The city fell behind, and smooth green fields stretched before me. At the Mound the fields were divided with hedgerows, just as they were at home. And many of the English settlers had built houses in the English style—wattle-and-daub cottages. It was almost like galloping back to Wooden Box.

Mary greeted me with a hug, and John hurtled himself into my arms.

"Hello, John," I said. "Have you caught a camel yet?"

"Not yet, Miss Mima. But I caught a toad at the pond. Mother said it was the largest toad she had ever seen."

"And so it was," Mary confirmed.

"I put it to live in our cellar," John continued. "Would you like to see him, Miss Mima?"

"I cannot wait," I replied.

Mary asked her mother-in-law to listen for the baby as I tied up the horse. We set off across the fields to the brick home Samuel was building half a mile away. John scampered ahead.

"The baby is poorly," said Mary as we walked.

"I'm sorry."

"It's the chills and fever. Curse this wretched climate. The river breeds disease." Her voice was hard.

"Many in town are also ill."

"I cannot sleep at night for worry," she admitted. "I lie in bed and listen to Elizabeth breathe."

I took her hand, remembering her hysterics when John was lost on the ship. "She will get better."

As we drew close to the new house, I could see the brickwork was finished, and Samuel was working on the roof. He climbed down the ladder when he saw us approaching. John ran into Samuel's arms, and Samuel laughed. "Afternoon, Miss Mima," he said. "How do you like our roof?"

"It is tall enough for John, I see."

"Yes," he grinned.

"And baby Elizabeth."

His eyes turned sober at the mention of the baby. "How is she, Mary?"

"She continues the same," said Mary. "She is napping now."

John scampered off to play under the nearby trees, his toad forgotten. "I hope you will come and visit us in the house when it is finished," Samuel said.

"When do you plan to move?"

"My parents say the weather will turn in mid-September. We plan to be in before then."

"Cold weather sounds nice on such a day," said Mary. She tugged on her bodice, which was soaked with sweat.

"And yet you'll be glad of the warm bricks when it comes," said Samuel.

"Miss Mima! Mother! Come and see!" John's voice rang from the woods.

"Not another toad," said Mary.

"What is it, John?" I called. I walked toward the woods. The field was filled with prairie grass and wildflowers. In time, I knew, it would be cleared for a garden and crops, but now it was wild and reminded me of the glades around the Box.

Mary followed me. I came upon John first. He was bent over, examining something on the ground.

As I drew closer, I searched the grass, wondering what animal he had trapped. But whatever it was lay very still.

Soon I stood beside him and bent over too. John brushed the grass aside. Hidden in the grass was a small nest. A fragment of blue shell remained inside. I leaned forward and lifted the delicate bowl in my hands. It was amazingly intricate. Tiny sticks and grasses, woven with precision, held together with mud. A corner of the nest was crushed. I looked up at the tall poplar tree next to us. The branches were high above the rooftop of the new house. "It must have fallen," I said, my eyes searching the branches to guess from where it might have tumbled.

"What about the baby bird?" asked John.

I turned to look at him and realized his eyes were wet with tears.

"I'm sure the baby is fine," I said. "See the eggshell? It probably flew away long before the nest fell down."

"Who knocked it down?" he asked, pouting.

"Probably the wind," I said. "I'm sure the baby bird is fine, John."

Mary caught up with us. She took in the nest and John's tears at a glance.

"The mother bird did not build it right," said John. "She did not keep the baby safe."

"Of course she did," said Mary. She hugged him. "Mothers always do."

"Now the baby can't go home," he said, looking up at the tree.

I followed his eyes. Such a long, long way. Such a shaky, slender tree.

Mary picked him up and carried him back to the house. "The baby can't go home," he sobbed against his mother's shoulder. "The baby can't go home."

I remained behind, still clutching the broken nest, turning it over and over in my hands. And suddenly I wanted to cry right along with him.

CHAPTER TWENTY-SIX

*I*n late August, our neighbor Sister Beth Ann bustled over, full of news. She carried more corn bread and a newspaper. "Thank you," I said, as I took the bread from her.

"You're welcome, my dear." She scurried into the kitchen. While her back was turned, I scowled at the corn bread for Mother's benefit.

Mother tried to look disapproving, but the corners of her mouth twitched suspiciously.

Lovely golden chicken feed, I thought, as Sister Beth Ann settled herself with great ado on a chair and rustled her newspaper, the latest issue of the *Nauvoo Neighbor.*

"Such news, dears, such news," Beth Ann said. "You never will guess. But try, dears, do try."

Mother and I looked at each other. "We simply cannot," said Mother. "Satisfy our curiosity, Sister Beth Ann."

"Not a guess? Well, then, I'll tell you. Brother James Emmett has returned!"

Mother and I exchanged another glance. "Brother Emmett?" said Mother, politely.

I stifled a yawn and thought perhaps I might see to another corset. Sewing seemed more and more entertaining by the moment.

"Yes. Isn't that remarkable, dears? He is back. And now look at this!" She shook the newspaper excitedly.

Mother went towards her and read where Sister Beth Ann pointed. "Hurrah for California," read Mother.

"Some folks in Nauvoo won't understand. They won't realize the connection. But I do. I know exactly what is going on. They can't pull the wool over my eyes. Do you see?"

"Yes," said Mother. "Rather, no. Sister Beth Ann, I'm afraid I do not see. Who is James Emmett and what does he have to do with this song?"

I edged my way toward the stairs. Even sock darning seemed preferable to this conversation.

"They'll be going to California. They will. In no time at all."

"Who will?" asked Mother. Honestly, she had the patience of a saint.

"Why, all of them. Brigham Young, the apostles, their families, and anyone who cares to join them. They are going to leave this country with all of its prejudices. Go somewhere the people of God can be free."

I stopped. Rooted to the floor. "Do you mean that will be the end of this?" I blurted. "They will leave Nauvoo? Abandon the city to the mobs?"

Sister Beth Ann looked around as if she had only just remembered that I was there. "Well, no," she said. "I suppose some will have to stay here. To see to the temple and keep up the city. But those who want to leave this accursed climate with its wicked neighbors can leave. This nation rejected God when they killed the Prophet, and now their day of vengeance will come."

I crossed the room and took the paper from her hands. I read:

> The upper California,
> O that's the place to be;
> It lies between the mountains,
> And the great Pacific sea.
> With a climate pure as Naples,
> And budding liberty,
> O clear away the rubbish,
> And let us there be free.

"So that is their plan?" I asked. My voice shook. I struggled to control it. "Everyone will just leave? Leave the temple, leave the city, leave all the people who have forsaken their homes to come to this place? They followed their leaders, and now they will desert them?"

Sister Beth Ann was flustered. "Well, I'm sorry, dear. I never dreamed. It's not like that, Miss Mima. Our leaders won't abandon us. We can join them if we like."

"If we like? If we like to spend our whole life wandering after them in the wilderness, waiting for them to find us a home?" I looked at Mother sharply. "No, thank you."

Mother sat stunned, looking from me to Sister Beth Ann and back again. "Mima," she called to me. But I did not want to hear what she was going to say. I ran from the room, my words hard and solid between us.

CHAPTER TWENTY-SEVEN

The weeks that followed seemed to show that Sister Beth Ann had been wrong. I heard little about California, and Nauvoo seemed peaceful and complacent in those last lazy weeks of summer. In September the days were still warm and muggy. But the evenings began to grow cool and brisk, with air so crisp you could snap it if you tried. The trees around the river began to turn, spots of red and orange touching their boughs. Occasionally I heard whispers of the leaders going west, but they seemed to be idle tales spread by the town gossips. I was relieved. Although I had little love for Nauvoo, I could not stand the thought of moving again. So Mother and I stocked the root cellar with potatoes and apples, carrots and onions. I looked at the frame boards of our house and hoped they would hold a winter's wind at bay.

Mary's house was finished. They moved in the second week of September and held a party to celebrate. Mother sewed us both new gloves for the occasion.

"Come along, Mima. You don't want to keep your friend waiting," she said.

"Here I am." I was wearing my brown silk dress. It was my only party dress that would still look clean by the time we arrived at Mary's.

"I can see the tops of your shoes in that gown," Mother said. "How you grow, child. I will have to let it out yet again."

"Then I will have to slouch tonight. It cannot be helped. It is the only decent option."

We piled into the carriage of the Dickinsons, friends of Mother's who were also going to the party.

When we arrived, the new house was lit up with candles and a cheery fire. Mary and Samuel greeted us at the door and welcomed us into their parlor. It would have been considered small by the Box's standards, but now that I was becoming used to Nauvoo's houses, the parlor seemed grand. They had decorated with a rug, split oak chairs, a tidy table, and a settee that had come from St. Louis. Vases of flowers sat around the room, and the table was topped with cakes, biscuits, and puddings.

"This is lovely, Mary," I said as I hugged my friend.

"Thank you. You will sing for us tonight, won't you?"

"Of course, if you like."

Most of the guests were from the Mound. Mother found a woman who was also from Leicestershire, only an hour's journey from the Box.

I recognized the Forsgrens from the ship. They had settled in town, and their English had greatly improved.

I had not seen Will for many weeks. I caught sight of his curly head and felt my pulse pick up. He approached and nodded; I curtseyed in return.

"Good evening, Miss Mima," he said.

"Good evening," I replied.

"Sing with me?" Will asked. I flushed at his bold words, just as I had on the ship months ago.

"Very well," I said. "What shall I sing?"

"Do you know 'Hurrah for California'?" he asked.

I gave him a hard look. "No, I do not."

"Same's a pity." I saw the laughter in his eyes and realized he was teasing me.

"I prefer 'God Save the Queen,'" I said blandly.

He laughed. "I see these months in Nauvoo have not tempered you. Nor converted you, either."

"Nor are they likely to."

"Why would God waste a lovely voice on such an obstinate Gentile as yourself?" His black eyes danced with mirth.

"That is simple, Mr. Farndon." I tipped my face toward his. "He has sent me to call the rest of you to repentance."

"When you sing, you nearly convince me."

I turned away so he would not see my blush.

There really wasn't space for dancing, but the guests pushed the furniture to the farthest corners of the room. Couples filed onto the floor for the quadrille.

Will began a lilting dance tune on his violin, and I joined him, the staccatos of his notes playing against the edges of my own.

The dancers laughed as they bumped into each other and occasionally the observers as well.

Heat rose from our bodies, and soon the room was an eerie mixture of heated bodies, music, and firelight. The rhythm pulsed, and I could feel my own heartbeat rise.

I stole a glance at Will's face. Beads of sweat clung to his forehead and slicked his dark hair, turning it full black. His eyes were closed, and he held his violin tenderly against his cheek. Adoration was full on his face, as if he were caressing his instrument. I blushed again at my thoughts. What would Mother think of me? I turned so I could not see his expression. But his melodies coursed through me, and I could still see the look on his face, pure exultation imprinted in my mind.

As the hours went on, it seemed to me that dark whispers began in the corners of the room. Those who were not dancing would go to the corners, dip into the secrets, and then come back to the dance floor. I could not hear the whispers, but between the songs, I thought I heard a whisper of "plural marriage" and then a moment later, "violence." I sang louder, trying with all my heart to drown out the fearsome words.

A young man I recognized from the Mound came toward me and bowed. "Will you dance, Miss Mima?" Suddenly all I wanted was the relief that dancing brings. And I could not stand next to Will a moment longer. I curtseyed low and accepted.

Dancing felt divine. I turned and stamped with fervor. Twisting and moving my body was a sweet release. As we danced the two-step, I let go of the tension I had felt standing next to Will. I danced out my frustration with Mother, the fear of violence, the longing for home. Tension began to ebb from my body, and I felt the music moving through me, begging me to follow. My partner was a fine dancer, but I would have danced with Brigham Young himself at that moment. Will's violin played on, and I was lost in his song.

Then faintly, it seemed the violin was accompanied by a low rhythmic percussion. At first I thought it was my heart's beating, but the noise grew louder and louder, and though it seemed familiar, I could not place it. I looked around the room, expecting to see an exotic instrument. By then the noise seemed to come from the very floor beneath us.

Constant. Heavy. Falling over and over. Like a pounding hand.

Samuel stepped to the door. Opened it. Peered out. One by one, people stopped dancing. Will's song still played as I stepped behind Samuel in time to see a horseman ride past. The horse and rider were a dark arrow shot through the night. A full and reckless gallop. Under cover of darkness. Headed toward Nauvoo.

My eyes strove with the night, trying to detect movement, but all now seemed still. Then Samuel flung the door wide and moved down the steps. He pointed in the opposite direction, the direction from which the rider had come. "Look," he said, his voice a whisper.

I followed his gaze. There in the black distance, an orange light shimmered on the horizon. The edges of the light were ragged and fierce. They clawed and raged at the sky, trying to burn up the hovering moon.

"Camp Creek settlement is on fire," Samuel said.

Women stifled screams. My dance partner stood stunned. Mother crossed the room and stood beside me. Will must have stopped playing sometime. He stood with his violin in his hands, uncertain what to do.

Samuel turned to me. "Mima, will you take Mary and the children to Nauvoo? I will go and see what help is needed."

I looked at Brother Dickinson. "Of course we can take them," he said. Others with carriages offered their assistance as well.

I reached for Mary, but she clutched at her husband. "Come with us, Samuel. Do not go. They will kill you, too."

"I'm sure the mob has fled, Mary, but there will be many suffering. Go with Mima. I will come for you tomorrow."

Mary turned away, her shoulders slumped.

I released Mother's hand and helped my friend with her cloak. Mother gathered clothing for the children. We loaded the Dickinsons' carriage with everything we could carry.

As I tucked in the last parcel, Will appeared beside me. "Miss Mima," he said, "my father and I will go with Samuel. Would you keep this safe for me?" He held his battered violin case lightly in his hands.

I caught my breath. "Has it truly come to this?" I said, understanding what he had placed in my hands.

"Perhaps not, but I'd rather not take the chance," he said.

"I will keep it safe, Mr. Farndon."

He bowed to me, never taking his eyes from mine. His eyes were deep pools of darkness. Kind and gentle darkness. I could drown in such eyes.

I curtseyed and cursed my wretched cheeks, as I felt the color rise again. I turned away, his instrument pressed into my dress. The case was warm against my body, as if the instrument inside, still hot from being played, had burned its way through the protective wood. I climbed into the carriage, and we rode away from the distant orange glow.

CHAPTER TWENTY-EIGHT

*S*ister Beth Ann heard the commotion of our arrival. We explained in short, whispered sentences. She took Samuel's parents to her home to sleep. I slid Will's violin under my dressing table, hoping it would not stay there for long. We tucked Mary and her children into Mother's bed. Mother and I squeezed into my own. We slept perhaps an hour? Two?

John's voice was clear in the darkness. "Mama, Mama, the baby is shaking." I nudged Mother next to me, but she was already awake. We listened for Mary's voice.

"What?" she said, struggling out of a dream.

"Shaking," John repeated.

Mother was up, lighting a candle before Mary was fully awake. "There now, Mary," Mother said. "Elizabeth will be fine."

Mary's hands fluttered for a moment like helpless birds. Then she snatched up the baby.

Mother's voice remained calm. "Young man, what excellent care you are taking of your little sister. You hop in with Mima and see if you can get back to sleep."

I pulled back the covers, and John jumped in beside me.

The baby *was* shaking. Her face was flushed, and I could see her shivering uncontrollably, even as Mary sought to calm her. Her little mouth chattered so hard I thought her tiny teeth would break.

Mother stood close by, helping Mary calm the infant. But her eyes rolled wildly, and she shivered violently. "It is the ague," Mary said. She slumped to the floor, the baby cradled on her knees. "She cannot leave me. Please don't leave me. Please don't let her leave me." Her words were frantic whispers. I held John close.

"She won't leave you," Mother said. "She'll never leave you. Children never leave their mothers."

"Yes, they do. They become cold and hard and go into the cold, hard ground where I cannot reach them."

Mother put a calm, steady arm around Mary and let her sob into her shoulder. Mother's other arm supported the baby so she would not fall. I marveled at Mother's strength. Sometimes I forgot how strong she was. And how kind.

"When did it happen?" Mother asked quietly. I held my breath. John clung to me.

Mary's eyes were closed. "A month before we left. Samuel wanted to leave before, but I refused. Then they both died." Tears streamed down her face. Her words were broken and ragged.

"My little James first, then William two days later. They coughed until all the air in their lungs was gone. Then I told Samuel we could go. I did not want to see their graves anymore. The cold, hard stone."

"There is little comfort in a gravestone," said Mother. "But they will never leave you."

"They have left me," Mary sobbed. "They are gone. Now Elizabeth will follow."

"They are yours," Mother said. "Forever."

"How can you say that? When your own husband is gone?"

"That is why I say it," Mother said. "They are with you still. Peace, Mary. Shhh. Find faith."

I held onto John and marveled at the words I had heard. My heart swelled for Mary. To lose two babies within days of each other. And then to come to this precarious frontier city from which safety had flown away. I could not imagine her grief. I could see that everything within her wanted to keep her children safe. Secure. Wasn't that what mothers were supposed to do? I thought of the fallen nest and John's words, "The mother did not build it right." But what if she *had* built it right? What if a storm came, so violent that all the mother's efforts were wasted?

Mother's words, too, were strange. What did she mean about Father? As a child I thought I could do what Mother said—know my father. Talk to him, listen to him, sense him somewhere in the sky. As a child I sang to him at the top of my lungs in the graveyard. Sometimes I felt he heard me. Sometimes I thought he sang with me. But as I grew older, I knew it was only a childhood fantasy. Slowly his memory grew hazy around the edges, fuzzy and faint.

Now all I remembered was being held in his warm arms, so safe and strong. I remembered the sound of his voice, the notes low and rumbling in his chest. And suddenly, the tune he sang came back to me. The soaring notes, the mournful longing put into music. It was the song Will had played. That was how I had recognized it on the ship. It had belonged to Father. I sang the words softly, whispering into the dark room.

> *The water is wide, I cannot cross o'er.*
> *And neither have I wings to fly . . .*

I could not remember the rest of the words. That haunting melody was Father to me.

I recalled the voice I heard in Liverpool saying, "How can you leave her alone?" Had it been Father? Had it been a devil? Had it been my own guilty conscience? I could not say. But I had not left her. I had followed her, so if it was Father, why had he deserted me? And how could Mother *know?*

"Mima," Mother said. I was startled back into the room. "We will say a prayer, and then I'd like you to fetch Doctor Norton."

I helped John kneel on the bed as Mother prayed. "Please, Lord," she said, "this infant is suffering. We ask Thee to have mercy on this child. Please heal her body and help her to sleep peacefully. We ask if it be possible that she will stay here with her brother and her mother who love her dearly. But if she must go, we trust her to Thee." Mary sobbed. "Thy will be done. In Jesus' name, amen."

I arose, tucked John back into the bed, and wrapped a shawl over my nightdress. I left Mary crying in Mother's arms.

When I returned with Doctor Norton, Elizabeth was sleeping peacefully, and Mary rested on Mother's lap. Mother slowly stroked her hair as if she were a small child. I looked at Mother's kind, worn hands, as familiar as bread. Her hands had comforted me so many times. Oddly, at that moment, I wanted to be Mary, to let Mother hold me. "My father died too," I wanted to say.

Doctor Norton examined Elizabeth. "This child is fine," he said. "What did you give her?"

Mother shook her head. "Nothing."

"She is fine," he said again. "Let her sleep."

We went to bed, even though the sky was beginning to lighten. I lay down next to John; Mother, beside Mary. In spite of exhaustion, for a time I could not sleep. Had Mother's prayer healed Elizabeth? Shock and ebbing emotion kept me awake, as the song played over and over in my head. *The water is wide, I cannot cross o'er . . .*

CHAPTER TWENTY-NINE

*W*e didn't stir until the sun was high in the sky. Elizabeth's color was good, her breathing easy. Samuel had not returned, but Mary seemed calm. She scarcely took her eyes off Mother. "He will come," she said to reassure herself.

Mother nodded.

The next evening, when Samuel still had not returned, Mary grew quiet, her eyes often darting to the door. That night I heard her tossing and turning, trying to sleep.

The next day was Sunday. Mother left for a preaching meeting near the temple. Mary and I held a service at home with John and Elizabeth. When it was over, Mary sent John outside to feed the chickens. He loved the chickens.

"Mima," Mary said, "thank you for sharing your mother with me." She looked down at baby Elizabeth. "I hope you did not mind."

I did not know what to say. "I'm glad Mother could comfort you," I said at last.

"Thank you for taking care of John." Mary paused. "I'm sorry I did not tell you my secret before. I could not speak of the children I lost."

"It is fine," I said. But I wasn't sure that it was. How do you tell a friend that you wish they liked you best? That you wish they could trust you with their secrets? I was younger than Mary, but she had never made me feel as if that mattered. It seemed to matter now.

The door opened, and Mother entered, smiling. "Can you guess what I found outside, Mary?"

Samuel was filthy. I thought Mary would burst into tears, but her face was pale and calm. She simply crossed the room and threw her arms around him.

Mother and I fled to the kitchen. "There's someone here for you, John," I called into the garden.

John burst through the door and looked into the front room. "Papa!" He ran to his father.

Mother and I waited several minutes and returned to the parlor. Mary beamed and could scarcely drag her eyes from his face. I wondered if I would ever look at someone that way. I wasn't sure if the thought terrified me or thrilled me. Perhaps both.

We were dying for news, but he was starving. Mother gave him food, and he ate with Mary beside him, touching his arm from time to time as if to make sure he was still real.

When he finished, he sat back in his chair. "Sister Hough, how can we thank you? You have been so kind."

"You don't know the half of what we owe her," said Mary, rocking Elizabeth.

"Brother Samuel, we are as hungry for information as you were for bread," Mother replied.

"I will tell you what I can, although it's not a pretty tale." He shook his head. "When we arrived at Camp Creek, the mob was gone. They were men on horseback with their faces painted black. They set fire to houses, barns, fields, almost anything that would burn."

"Did anyone get hurt?" Mary asked.

"The mob roughed up a few men, but no one was killed, as far as we know."

"Those poor people," said Mother. "Winter is coming on, and now they've no place to live. What will they do?"

"They are not the only ones who need shelter. It appears the mobs actually started a few days ago at Morley's Settlement and Bear Creek in the south and then moved north to La Harpe and Camp Creek. More than a hundred houses have been burned."

"Where will all those people go?" asked Mother.

"Some have fled south to St. Louis, but we have brought most of them to Nauvoo with any food and clothing they could salvage. People are taking them in. Many are staying at the Music Hall." He looked at me. "All concerts have been cancelled for now."

"What do the mobs want?" I asked.

"They want us to leave Illinois. Just like in Missouri. They say there is no room for Mormons here. And it appears that they are going to win, Miss Mima."

"Is Brigham Young leaving?" asked Mother.

Samuel nodded slowly. "Brigham Young, all of the Twelve. They have promised that all Mormons will leave in the spring."

"All of us?" said Mary.

Samuel nodded, his eyes pained. "I'm sorry, Mary. I wanted that house to be our home for the rest of our days." He put his head in his hands.

I looked from Mother to Mary to Samuel, trying to grasp his words. "But where are we to go?"

Samuel lifted his head. "West. They are going to a wilderness where we can worship in peace. Perhaps northern California. Perhaps the Rocky Mountains. No one knows exactly where. Far from this country, where we have been hated and despised."

California? Anger coursed through my veins. "Well, *I* am not going to follow Brigham Young into the wilderness, looking for another Zion. I have had quite enough of Zion to last the rest of my life," I said. I looked at Mother as I spoke.

She flinched.

A few weeks passed, full of tension and questioning. We learned that Orrin Porter Rockwell, a Mormon, had killed a citizen of Warsaw in self-defense. The surrounding communities were outraged and demanded the Mormons' immediate removal.

Not many days later, Mary came to call. Mother was out settling our account with Abel Lamb. I was surprised to see my friend but greeted her warmly. I invited her inside and poured her a cup of tea.

"Mary, you braved the mob to visit me?" I teased.

But her face was serious. "I had to talk to you," she said.

"What is it?"

"A man who helped us with our house called earlier today. He is not a Mormon, and since we now plan to leave . . ." Mary sighed. "We had not seen him for some time. But today he came by to say he felt it was his duty to tell us what is going on. He brought this newspaper published in Warsaw."

She drew the newspaper from the folds of her skirts. *The Warsaw Signal.* I knew Warsaw as the name of a town some fifteen miles from Nauvoo.

I glanced at the headline "More Mormon Delusions" and scanned the page. The paper accused Brigham Young and other leaders of the Church of villainy, dishonesty, and infidelity. My hand was suddenly shaky, and I dropped the paper into my lap. "What did Samuel say about this?"

She shook her head. "He said they are lies made up by those who want to destroy the Mormons." Her face struggled to find the words. "But can it *all* be made up? What if some of it is true?"

I pressed Mary's hand. Her brick home would soon have to be abandoned, her children dragged off once again in search of . . . what? "I'm so sorry," I said, feeling it to be a ridiculously feeble response.

"Do you think your mother knows about these things?" Mary asked.

I shook my head. "I don't know. May I keep the newspaper?"

"Keep it," she said. "I have no eagerness for having it nearby."

That night I lay awake as the darkness grew deeper. The sky was black, covered over with heavy, stifling clouds. The newspaper lay hidden under the mattress. My mind spun. I could not sleep. Rumors and fragments flitted through my head. The temple, nearly finished in its loveliness, tainted by allegations of deception and counterfeiting and violence, and perhaps most awful of all, accusations of immorality. This city, supposed to be Zion, now seemed anything but peaceful and pure. True, I knew my neighbors and Church leaders to be kind people of integrity, and yet . . . I longed to show the newspaper to Mother, but I wasn't sure if I could. Would she deny the claims? Would she blame Mary for showing me? It seemed impossible for us to talk openly about these things.

What could we do? Where should we go? We could not go back to England. I could not go on into the wilderness. I felt trapped between two continents, floating somewhere in the middle of the harsh Atlantic, pulled by every wave. I played out scenarios again and again until my mind was hazy and my nerves were frayed. I remembered the flash of lightning during the storm at sea. Once again, I could not see the way ahead. Where was the flash now? Why had God preserved us only to abandon us once on shore?

I could not make sense of it. I could not think my way out. I belonged nowhere. Was there anywhere on earth I truly wanted to be?

I thought of Providence House, the windows streaming with sunlight, the rooms filled with song, the closet where I practiced writing my name on the walls until Mother found me. The creaky fourth stair that I had jumped on again and again. The dining room, where we had entertained friends—Charlotte's family, Mother's sewing friends, my music teacher.

But Father's other daughter lived there now. Providence House as I loved it existed only in my mind. I wanted to remember every detail so that it would never fade. But in reality, it was already gone.

Gone because of Mother, with her crazy knowing and maddening silences. I wished I had somehow forced her to stay. I wished I had stayed in Liverpool with George. Regret burned within me. Mother had made decision after decision without regard for my feelings. And I had allowed her to. True, I was young, and I was supposed to obey. But whether she cared to notice or not, I had become a young woman. And I needed to protect us both. It was time to act before we ended up huddled in some camp on the edge of the wilderness. I tried to listen for Father's voice, directing me, chastising me. Anything. But there was only silence and darkness. Mother and Father had failed me. On that dark night it seemed that even God had failed me. I would have to find a path of my own.

The next morning, I rose early and walked through the streets of Nauvoo. The city was bustling as people built wagons, gathered supplies, and prepared to leave. From time to time I passed Nauvoo citizens who had now become watchmen. They carried rifles and patrolled the river and bluffs above the city, prepared to sound the alarm of war, if necessary. I eyed the cold steel of the watchman's rifle and shivered.

Before I could change my mind, I continued to the docks. They were oddly quiet. At the office a clerk came towards me.

"May I help you?"

"Yes. I would like to book passage to St. Louis."

"How many passengers?"

"Two."

"Date of travel?"

I swallowed. "Two weeks from today."

"That will be fourteen dollars."

I opened the silk purse Charlotte had given me at Providence House long ago. Little had I known at the time that she had handed me freedom. "I have only English coins," I told the clerk.

"That is fine," he said.

A moment later he handed me change and two receipts for passage. I thanked him and left the office. As I neared home, I walked more and more slowly. My idea had seemed so brave and valiant last night in bed; it seemed foolish and ridiculous by the light of day. Would Mother come with me? Between her daughter and her religion, who would she choose? Did I want to know? As I neared the house on Parley Street, I remembered walking home to Providence House after Vespers so long ago. That night I had loathed the thought of going home because I did not want to hear what Mother might tell me. Now I did not want to go home because I had a secret I did not know how to tell her.

CHAPTER THIRTY

Mother was sewing, of course. She sat next to the window, using the afternoon sun to finish another corset. I was sick of corsets and wished again for the lace we used to sell in England. But there was little need for lace in Nauvoo where many people could not buy food. Perhaps that would be different in St. Louis. She raised her eyes when I entered, smiling the half-smile she had been wont to give me of late.

"Where have you been, daughter?"

I hesitated. Then I said, "I am determined to leave Nauvoo."

"We will all be leaving in time."

"But I mean to leave soon." My hands were cold, and I felt blood rushing to my head. I crossed the room and sat down.

"Where will you go?"

"I mean to go to St. Louis. I have heard it is a large city, with seminaries and music halls."

"And you mean to go alone?"

"Oh, Mother, will you come with me? I left Providence House to join you here. We cannot return to England, but perhaps we could open a small shop in St. Louis."

Mother's eyes softened, and her face relaxed. She laid her sewing beside her chair and looked at me. "You gave up much to come with me, Mima. I am sorry you have regretted it so."

I held my breath.

"I have watched you each day grow further from me, until I felt I had only the shell of you left, while your heart was still in the Box."

My face burned. "Yes, I have regretted it," I said.

"But what of my faith? My religion? What of them?"

I had waited for this question. "Perhaps you will have to choose. Between my home and you, I chose you. Who will you choose, Mother?"

She crossed the room to sit next to me and took my hand in hers. Her hand felt warm and strong. "Daughter, I will always choose you. I believe that *is* choosing God. He wants me to care for you. I was willing to leave you in Liverpool only because I believed it would be best for you. But to have left you there would have been to leave my heart across the ocean."

Sobs welled up from deep inside. Mother held me, as she had held Mary. It was pure comfort and safety in her arms. And finally, I felt the decision I had made and regretted bitterly had been the right decision after all. I was glad I had come. Glad I was beside Mother, wherever we were.

When my sobs calmed, Mother stroked my face. A surge of affection for her welled up in my heart, and I wanted to have no secrets between us. "I must show you something," I said. I rushed from the room and fetched the newspaper from under my mattress. I returned and handed it to her. She took the paper without a word and read the front page through without comment.

Her eyes were thoughtful when she raised them to meet mine. "Do you know who publishes this newspaper?" she asked.

I shook my head.

"Thomas C. Sharp," she said. "He is a bitter enemy of Joseph Smith and the Mormons. There are many who feel that his newspaper led to the Prophet's death."

I shivered. "But surely some of it is true?" I asked.

"There may be some truth to it," she said. "Nauvoo is in a state of tumult, there can be no question about that."

"So perhaps . . . " I began.

Mother's face was calm. "Faith is something that almost always seems strange to those who don't believe the same doctrines." She hesitated, searching for the right words. "When I'm at church meetings and when I pray, I feel peace, I feel joy." Her eyes held mine with intensity. "I have found I must rely upon my feelings when the Spirit speaks to my heart."

I knelt next to her, burying my head in her lap. I struggled to understand my feelings.

Mother stroked my hair gently. "Mima, I know Brother Brigham to be a wise leader with integrity. He is not the kind of man this newspaper portrays him to be."

I remembered the few times I had seen Brigham Young. He had struck me as a man of sincerity. The shrill accusations of the paper began to seem frantic and implausible.

But still Nauvoo was a place I did not wish to be. Mother's hands were warm upon my back.

"There are many Latter-day Saints in St. Louis, daughter. It may be that we can both find peace in that city. We will go together."

Her words filled me with joy. I nodded, so happy I could not speak. The sun streaming through the windows bathed the room with light.

Two weeks later we stood on the deck of a steamer bound for St. Louis. This time no crowd had welcomed the riverboat when it arrived in Nauvoo. The city had a brooding, oppressive air. Although it was only October, the air was chilly, the days were growing shorter, and the whole city was preparing to be abandoned. Homes had been turned into shops where wagons were being assembled, axles greased, wagon covers sewn, and food stored in barrels.

Mary and Samuel did not come to the landing to see us off. Instead, they had come to the house on Parley Street the night before. Mary bade us a tearful good-bye. "I hope to join you in St. Louis. If I can convince Samuel, we will be there by spring." I hugged my friend, wondering if we would ever meet again.

Sister Beth Ann sent us off with corn bread, and several other friends of Mother's gave us preserves and dried, salted meat. We were loath to accept their gifts, as we were more concerned for them than for us.

The only person I did not say good-bye to was Will. I had asked Samuel about him, and he shrugged. "Brother Farndon and Will helped for three days at Camp Creek and then departed. I have heard that Brother Farndon decided to go back to England to the rest of his family. But no one seems sure."

"Will cannot have left. I have his violin," I told Samuel.

"Then keep it," he said. "If he knows you have it, I'm sure he will contact you when he's able. If I hear from the lad, I will write you in St. Louis."

The thought of Will separated from his violin somehow made my heart sadder than all the stories of suffering I had heard since the mobbing began. I packed the violin case carefully in a trunk with my most cherished possessions: my sheet music, the quilt from my bed at Providence House, the daguerreotype of Father, and Charlotte's silk purse.

The last glimpse I had of Nauvoo was the white temple rising above the collection of frame and brick houses. They would all soon be abandoned. Strangely, even as the Mormons prepared to leave the city, they increased their work on the temple. They hoped to have it completed before they departed, but I could not imagine why it was still important. The temple and the collection of homes surrounding it now seemed fragile and precarious as they disappeared around the bend of the Mississippi River. I looked back at the city for a time and then turned to look downstream.

CHAPTER THIRTY-ONE

hortly after we passed the point where the Illinois River joined the Mississippi, the city of St. Louis came into sight. A cluster of passengers stood at the deck to see the town that awaited them. A woman called Sister Liza stood beside me. She was leaving Nauvoo to rejoin her husband in St. Louis. She had grown up there and spoke of that city as I would speak of the Box.

Like Nauvoo, St. Louis was laid out on a bluff. But this city was much older and more established than Nauvoo. From the river it looked as if the buildings had been lined up just for our eyes. Steamboats puffed along the busy levee. Even from a distance, the white, lime-coated buildings gave the city a bright, clean appearance.

Sister Liza pointed. "There is the steeple of the Old Cathedral.

You will love St. Louis, Miss Mima. The city was settled by French settlers nearly one hundred years ago, so it feels more European than American. You will be right at home."

At the mention of home I immediately thought of Providence House. I doubted anything in St. Louis could compare with those memories, and I eyed the city dispiritedly. As we drew closer, we could see the bustle and commotion of a busy city. Carriages, horses, people, and boats moved along the wharf. St. Louis was much larger than Nauvoo. It was a frontier city, but the churches and government buildings were impressive. We drew into port, and I exclaimed at the enormous levee, which was lined with cobblestones and warehouses.

Sister Liza smiled. "The city plans to add gas streetlamps next year. Won't that be a sight? Can you imagine the city lit up and glistening in the water?"

When we stepped off the boat, Sister Liza greeted her husband and turned back to me. "Won't you join us?" she invited. Mother and I gratefully climbed into their carriage.

In spite of myself, I was thankful for the Mormons' help. They seemed to have an intricate network of assistance. Brother Lewis was a portly man with a gray beard. Sister Liza had dark hair and ash-colored eyes.

"Welcome to St. Louis," Brother Lewis said as the carriage started off. "What is the news of Nauvoo?"

"Ill," said Mother. "All is talk of leaving in spring, with no clear idea of where they may be headed."

"Brother Brigham will lead them to safety, I am sure," said Brother Lewis.

"Will you be joining him?" I asked.

"Perhaps in time," he replied. "We are comfortable in St. Louis and loath to leave it for the wilderness. You will find many Mormons in St. Louis. The Saints here enjoy pleasures and comforts not to be found in Nauvoo. We number more than fifteen hundred."

"So many?" said Mother. "How can that be, when the Mormons were driven from Missouri? Didn't the governor issue orders for extermination?"

"Yes," said Brother Lewis, "but that was rural Missouri. Most citizens of St. Louis pride themselves on being open-minded. We have colleges that admit women, we settle Irish immigrants in the Kerry Patch, and we even permit Mormons to practice their religion. Most people in the city think what happened in Independence was pure rural ignorance."

"Is there an Anglican church here?" I asked. I didn't wish to pretend to be a Mormon.

Brother Lewis looked surprised. "Yes, of course. There is Christ Church parish yonder." I looked out the window of the carriage and saw a small chapel slide past our view.

Sister Liza said, "In her letter, your mother said you were interested in music. Just ahead is Phillips Music store. It is a meeting place for everyone in the city interested in musical arts."

"Thank you," I said, looking out the window at the storefront close to the lovely cathedral I had seen from the river.

Sister Liza turned to Mother. "You will be staying near Market Street?" she asked.

Mother nodded.

"A good choice for business," said Brother Lewis.

Mother had arranged through friends in Nauvoo to take an apartment on the border of the French quarter of the city. I loved the narrow cobbled streets that reminded me so much of the streets at the Box. The apartment was in a sturdy brick building. I thought of the flimsy frame walls of the house in Nauvoo and knew we would be grateful for the bricks in a few more weeks when winter began in earnest. It had room for a shop with a separate entrance and a kitchen and cellar out back. Mother was thrilled. I had my own small bedroom and was equally happy. But when Mother saw the rent amount her forehead puckered in worry. "You will have to sew as well as sing, Mima, to stay in this city."

"Yes, Mother," I said, with a sigh.

Before the Lewises departed, Mother asked Sister Liza, "Please tell us. What linens will do well here? In Nauvoo we sewed corsets, and in England, lace."

"The city truly could use another skilled dressmaker. And laces are quite fashionable," said Eliza.

"Cheers for St. Louis," I said. "I am full sick of corsets."

"Mima!" said Mother when the Lewises departed. "What has gotten into you? You are beginning to sound as forward as a frontier girl. I've half a mind to take you straight back to England."

"Oh, would you truly, Mother?" I asked.

"You are impossible," she said. But her eyes were kind.

I stepped to the window and looked out at St. Louis. The city streets were teeming with life. People and horses and carriages. Soon there would be gas street lamps. The city was just beginning. It was on the brink of something wonderful, and I hoped to grow right along with it. Giddy with the thrill of success from my actions, I couldn't wait to unpack our things into this new life. I opened a window to let in the noise from the street below.

"In the spring I will plant the flowers from Providence House in pots on the balcony," I said, clapping my hands. The seeds and clippings had been packed carefully in my trunk.

Mother smiled at my glee and began organizing lengths of fabrics into carefully arranged rows: silks, muslins, scrim, cotton prints, laces, and threads. She stacked them into piles, ordered, neat, and tidy.

CHAPTER THIRTY-TWO

*B*etween Mother's friends in the Mormon church and my friends in the Anglican, Mother's dressmaking business started slowly but grew steadily. She found a store to carry corsets as a constant source of income, but within a few months, we were able to leave off the corsetry work and focus on dressmaking. Mother's customers paid with hard currency, too, something we had not seen during our time in Nauvoo. Laces were popular, and once again Mother carried Berlin work with her. She organized her shop much as she had at Providence House, and as she moved from project to project, the silver chatelaine at her waist tinkled, a familiar sound of home.

For the first month, Mother needed every moment of my time setting up shop and sewing. I had no time to sing or explore. But finally one afternoon in early November, Mother set me free with a nod. "You have worked hard these weeks, Mima. Take the afternoon for your own, then. I'll finish up."

"Thank you, Mother," I said, kissing her on the cheek. My affection for her had returned with the hope I'd found in St. Louis.

I gathered my cloak and hat and rushed to the street. The air was crisp and cold. Brilliantly colored leaves lay upon the raised wooden sidewalks like splashes of dry paint. I loved the bustle and busyness of the city. Ladies in fine hats and cloaks peered from closed coaches, and gentlemen nodded in top hats. I passed chimney sweeps with blackened faces and maids carrying brightly wrapped parcels. Everyone seemed to be going somewhere with a purpose. I walked to the end of the street and turned onto Market Street. There was no question of where I wanted to go. My feet stopped directly in front of a brick building, and I looked up at the sign. Phillips Music Store. I took a deep breath and opened the door.

A small bell chimed as I entered. The shop smelled of lavender, and I thought of Charlotte. My eyes took in the instruments displayed around the room. Violins, cellos, horns, and a harp stood in one corner. One wall was lined with shelves of sheet music. Another held music stands and cases, and in the back of the store was a walnut pianoforte. My fingers ached to touch it. Would I even remember how to play?

A woman with steely gray hair swept up in a chignon came from the back. She was dressed simply in black silk, exuding elegance.

"May I help you?" she asked.

I did not know what to say. "My name is Mima Hough, and I . . .

want to sing," I said lamely. "I was told . . ." I could not finish the sentence.

She gave me an appraising glance. "You were told to come here?"

I nodded, miserably.

"Well, then," she said. "I am Madame Leonora Phillips. Let me hear you sing. Do you play the pianoforte?"

I nodded. She gestured to the instrument. The wood was intricately carved. I sat down and stretched my hands over the ivory keys. They felt cool and smooth beneath my fingertips. My eyes followed the keys up the keyboard, lovely in their ordered, perfect rows. Three black keys in a cluster, then two white, followed by two black. Over and over all the way up the keyboard. As familiar as home.

I played "Flow Gently, Sweet Afton." At first I sang hesitantly, nervous as I was to have her hear my song. But soon I was lost in the melody and forgot she stood beside me.

When I was finished, I looked up at her. Her face was impassive, and I squirmed on the bench. At last she smiled. "Mima, I see that you can indeed sing. You have talent."

Elation coursed through me. But she held up her hand in a gesture of caution.

"However, many people have talent. Talent is not enough. Talent is only useful if one is willing to work very hard. Training one's voice is difficult work. Are you willing to do it?"

"Yes," I said. "I am willing." I lifted my face and met her eyes directly.

"Then I believe I can help you," Madame Leonora said.

Madame Leonora did help me. Soon every afternoon Mother could spare me I spent at the music store. If Madame Leonora was busy, I browsed through the sheet music. When she was available, I would talk with her about music. "Do you have any new arrangements by Beethoven?" I would ask.

And she would often say, "Yes, Mima. Come and see the score."

When business was slow and she was not with customers, I would take a piece of music to her. "Madame Leonora, is this choir piece best sung legato or staccato?" I would use any excuse to attract her attention because soon she would be playing for me as I sang, and then she would critique.

"It is breath support, Mima. All in the breath," she told me the first time we worked together. "A singer must have a diaphragm as strong and supple as an athlete's. You are taking your listener across a river, and you use your breath to hold him afloat. Clumsy singers allow the listener to bob up and down, sustaining one moment, dropping him the next. The listener does not want to be plunged into the stream because you have forgotten to breathe. It takes strength to hold him up. Engage your muscles to hold him above the water. Do not let him slip. The phrases must be seamless, until you place him peacefully at the edge of the bank.

"Here. I will show you what I mean." She picked up a heavy book and pushed the spine into my stomach. "Now push the book back with your diaphragm, Mima."

I tightened my stomach muscles and tried to push against the book.

"Now breathe in," she instructed. I did so, expanding my diaphragm into the book spine.

"Yes, that is correct. That is the feeling with each breath. But between breaths, you must not let the book sink in. Now sing."

She continued pushing the book into my stomach while I endeavored to sing "Come, Thou Fount of Every Blessing." All my effort was concentrated on breathing. I gave little thought to the form of each word. By the end of the song I was exhausted, and my stomach muscles ached with fatigue. I placed a hand on the pianoforte for support.

"You see?" Madame Leonora nodded, pleased. "That is what true singing feels like. When you are singing correctly, it takes your whole body, your whole heart, and your whole mind. Between breathing, diction, notes, and dynamics, your brain is set to spinning. And yet you must smile, pretending that it costs but little effort. That is the illusion of art."

"But I can hardly sing for five minutes that way. What must I do to strengthen my stomach?"

"You must practice singing properly. You must exercise your lungs with walking. And you must hit your stomach thirty times each morning and night." She showed me how to lightly hit my tightened stomach with balled hands.

As I left the store, my muscles throbbed with pain, but I could not stop smiling. I was a part of the world I had longed for. It was here, ahead of me. I prayed that nothing would pull it from my grasp.

CHAPTER THIRTY-THREE

*P*hillips Music Store truly was the hub of the music world in St. Louis. I was accepted into the Christ Church cathedral choir. The cathedral was a beautiful building with glimmering stained glass, purple velvet cushions, and wood trim made of carved black walnut. Once again I sang for services—Compline, Mass, and Evensong. Familiar and ordered, just like the piano keys, white, black, white. As I became more comfortable in St. Louis, I hung onto the pieces that were like home. Familiar pieces. It all seemed too perfect to last. I lived in fear that I would wake up one day, and it would end.

While we worked together, Madame Leonora told me about the newest stars performing on the St. Louis stage and the songs that were being composed. She often let me play the pianoforte. "It is good for business," she told Mr. Phillips, but really she could see how much I loved it. Seated at the pianoforte, I could pretend I was at home. I thought of Will, separated from his instrument. My heart ached for him, wherever he was.

Each time I performed a new song, Madame Leonora considered it with me. "You must study, Mima. Learn of each composer and the time in which he composed," she told me, tapping her fingers on the side of the pianoforte in time to an invisible rhythm.

"As a writer is influenced by the time and place in which he lives, as you cannot truly understand a book unless you know of the author, so it is with song," she continued. "You cannot understand a piece unless you know of the composer, the time he was responding to, and what he was trying to say."

Madame Leonora sat down beside me at the pianoforte, her fingers gliding gently over the surface of the keys. "For instance, when you sing Bach," she said, and here she nodded at me, expecting me to play.

I quickly found the keys and began the opening lines of a Bach prelude.

"Yes," she said, "but now recall that Bach was German, writing during the Baroque period for the harpsichord and organ. He was a master of the contrapuntal style, in which several melodies are played at once. Each one must be expressed in the piece, heard clearly and distinctly as you play."

She raised her hand, as if conducting me, and I played the opening lines of the prelude again, struggling to keep each note slightly separate, while also trying to emphasize the musical phrases that echoed back and forth between the left and right hands. "It is hard to think of both detaching and blending at the same time," I said as I left off playing. I smoothed my dress in frustration.

"Yes," said Madame Leonora, "but now consider that additionally, he was a cantor and vocal instructor and a deeply religious Lutheran. Most of his music was written for the worship service."

She leaned energetically toward me to emphasize her point. "When you play a piece by Bach, you need to pour that knowledge into the piece. Let us hear the awe and reverence he would have brought to it."

She motioned for me to play the opening of the prelude again. I closed my eyes, trying to capture awe. I thought of St. Peter's with its colored glass and spires, the ocean and its fathomless depths. The image of the limestone walls of Nauvoo's temple surprised me by rising unbidden. I leaned into the keys, trying to express a fragment of those feelings in my playing.

"Good," said Madame Leonora, keeping time with her hand. I struggled to infuse the piece: separate, yet together, full of awe.

"Excellent. You are beginning to capture it," said Madame Leonora. "Now, you must do the same with your voice, interpreting the piece for your audience."

Madame played for me, as I sang fragments of Bach, striving to express his thoughts and ideas through my sound. After singing the first line, Madame Leonora stopped playing and abruptly stood up. "One moment," she said, leaving the room. She returned a few minutes later holding a looking-glass and a candle.

I must have looked a picture of confusion, but she smiled and held the glass and the light close to my mouth. "Examine your throat position, my dear. Do you see your tongue, mounded high near the back? A beautiful tone is produced with an open throat."

I peered into the glass, noticing that my tongue, in fact, was neatly mounded near the back of my throat.

"Yawn," she instructed. I giggled at the silliness of the scene but did as I was told.

"Do you notice that when you yawn, your soft palate is elevated, and the tongue is lowered? This is what an open throat feels like and should be striven for every time you sing."

She held up the glass and light and instructed me to sing the opening phrase. I peered into the glass again. My tongue was lowered now, the tone came fuller and rounder, a much more operatic tone and more formal than I was used to.

"Yes," said Madame Leonora, "that is much better. Now seek for that each time you sing."

We practiced until my muscles ached, and Madame finally said, "Enough for today, Mima. You are keeping your promise to work hard."

As I walked home that afternoon, I played over and over in my head Madame Leonora's words about Bach and found myself wondering if I wrote a song, what would it be? And what would you need to know of me to understand it? The grief I felt for Father, for Providence House, for home? Or my coming to this new place, full of hopes to sing and study and grow? I could not imagine such a song that could hold grief and hope together in the same melody.

Mary and Samuel arrived in early spring. They had somehow sold their brick house and come to St. Louis to prepare for their journey west. Samuel was still determined to follow Brigham Young, but I hoped to convince my friends to stay in St. Louis.

They took an apartment on Locust Street, also near the French Quarter. Mother and I went to call. When I saw Mary again, she wrapped her arms around me. I took in her distinctive smile, her shining brown eyes.

"Mima, my friend," she said. "It is so good to see you."

"Yes," I replied, as she pulled me into the parlor. "I'm sure they miss their renegades in Zion. How can they ever manage without us?"

Mary smiled as she took my bonnet, but her face was serious. "It isn't Zion anymore, I'm afraid."

Mother and Samuel entered the room in time to hear Mary's remark. "We've read about Nauvoo in the papers. How much of it is true?" asked Mother.

"Things went from bad to worse after you left," Mary said with a shudder. "Many people simply left their homes without selling them at all. In February mobs forced most of the Saints to leave."

"In the middle of the winter?" I asked.

Mary nodded.

"The river froze over, which hardly ever happens," said Samuel. "But it made it so they could cross over more easily."

"We were able to stay longer than most, since our house was outside the city. Now the town mostly consists of the sick and elderly," said Mary.

"Where is Brigham Young?" I asked.

"Somewhere in Iowa Territory," said Samuel.

"Do they know where they will go?"

"West," he replied.

I shivered, imagining spending the winter in a flimsy tent. "There are many Saints in St. Louis," I said. "It is a lovely city, with many diversions."

"We have heard there are many iniquities here, too," said Samuel. "Gambling houses, liquor stores, and crime. We will stay only as long as necessary."

I sighed and took Mary's hand in my own.

"Come and help me," Mary said.

We left Samuel and Mother with the children and went to the kitchen, where Mary checked the bread baking on the hearth. "The counterfeiting charges were dropped after Brigham Young left," said Mary. "I believe they just wanted the Mormons to leave."

"It seems they got their way," I said sadly. "What of the rumors of plural marriage?"

"There may have been some truth to that," said Mary. "But what of you?" she asked, changing the subject. "How have you spent your time in this city?"

"With as little sewing and as much singing as I can manage," I replied. "The music store here is a center for musicians and singers all over the city. I am learning a great deal."

"And what of your social life? I was married when I was your age, you know. Are there any prospects?"

I shook my head. "No, no prospects. Even Will Farndon has disappeared, though I have his violin. Have you heard from him?"

Mary shook her head. "The last I heard was that his father had returned to England. Perhaps Will went with him. But you always said you wouldn't marry a Mormon. Or did his violin playing persuade you to change your mind?"

"His playing was divine," I said. "But . . ." I thought of Father dying, leaving Mother to raise me alone. I thought of Samuel pulling his wife and children across a wilderness. I did not wish to hurt Mary's feelings, but nothing I had seen of marriage made me crave it. "I wish only to sing," I said at last.

Her eyes searched my face, and she seemed to read some of the thoughts I would not say aloud. She pressed a finger to her chin and nodded thoughtfully.

A month later, I stood trembling in the shadows in the music store. Madame Leonora could read the fear on my face. "Breathe, my dear. You will do well. Remember all we have discussed, keep your throat open, support your breath, prolong the vowels, and articulate the consonants."

I nodded, snatching at the fragments of all we had studied together. That night I was to sing at a concert with some of the best musicians in St. Louis. And Madame was introducing me as her special vocal student. I desperately did not want to disappoint her. True, many had admired my voice, but I had really performed only in small places—Wooden Box, Nauvoo, and a ship upon the sea. What did such audiences know of training and music?

"Remember all these things," Madame continued, "and then relax completely. Forget anyone is listening to you. Express your love of music, and you will dazzle them."

I nodded, breathing deeply, still clutching to her arm.

She smiled indulgently, as if I were a small child. I realized I was holding to her like a survival raft. I relaxed my grasp and brushed imaginary wrinkles from my dress, which was green watered silk, a new gown Mother had made for the occasion.

"It is time, dear," Madame said, and her head resumed its regal posture. I followed her from the back room to the main section of the store, trying to look as calm as she did. She saw through me at a glance and offered me her arm. I smiled gratefully and let my gloved finger rest upon the inside of her elbow.

A large portion of the room had been cleared for the occasion. A small dais had been set up as a stage. A pianoforte stood next to it, and several other instruments were arranged on a nearby table. The room was resplendent with red velvet adorning the tables. One table was covered with cakes, dainties, and tarts. The room gleamed in the light of hundreds of candles set in large silver candelabra.

Elegant guests in evening gowns and tailored suits milled about the room, sipping champagne from crystal flutes and talking politely. I suddenly felt like a young girl in plaits.

"Ah," said one man with a black mustache, "here at last is the woman of the hour." Tall and stately with a well-trimmed coat, he bowed to Madame Leonora.

"Mr. Everton," said Madame Leonora. "So kind of you to join us," she replied with a nod. She drew me forward. "And this is Miss Mima Hough, who will flatter us with a solo this evening."

I dropped a curtsy, trying to seem grown up. "Pleasure to meet you, Mr. Everton."

He bowed again. "The pleasure is mine. I have heard Madame speak of her young and talented singer. I look forward to hearing your selection."

"Thank you," I stammered.

We passed onto the dessert table, greeting more guests along the way. Two women, their hair coiled fashionably and adorned with glittering gems, their dresses of expensive raw sprigged silks, cut fashionably, eyed me jealously when Madame introduced me.

"Ah, yes," said one of the women, her diamond earbobs shimmering in the candlelight. "Madame has been hiding you too long."

"Madame is too kind," I said, my cheeks turning pink once more.

"Perhaps," said her friend with a smile that was a bit cold.

"Miss Grace plays the pianoforte," Madame explained. "You will hear her tonight."

"I shall look forward to it," I said, but the woman only nodded.

Many of the men were handsome, so handsome they left me a bit dazzled and speechless. Mary's question of suitors echoed in my ears, and I blushed at the thought.

I met several more guests, too many to possibly remember all their names, but they were all elegant. Many, whose names I had heard in the newspaper and from Madame, were serious and successful musicians. Did I really belong amongst these glittering guests? We made our way to the dessert table, but I couldn't eat. I managed a sip of champagne and put the glass down.

At last Madame steered me toward the seats. She walked to the dais to welcome everyone and announce the concert order.

The distinguished man with the black mustache sang a beautiful rendition of "Open Thy Lattice, Love," a popular new song. He had a rich, throaty baritone that reminded me of melting butter.

Next a lovely woman with red twisting curls played a divine Chopin étude on the harp. It made me think of Providence House and the cabbage roses blooming in the garden, so peaceful and lyrical.

Miss Grace of the cold smile rose next and played a Bach cantata on the pianoforte. The number was executed flawlessly, and yet I noticed with some satisfaction that the performance was a bit austere and unfeeling for my taste.

But a moment later I was glad I had been distracted by Miss Grace's performance because Madame stood and introduced me as the newest member of their musical group, lately arrived from England and a talented singer with dedication and promise. I flushed at her praise, hoping to try to live up to it. I rose, walking awkwardly toward the dais, painfully aware of my audience.

Madame was to play the accompaniment on the pianoforte for me. I nodded to her, and she began the opening bars of "I Dreamt I

Dwelt in Marble Halls," a popular aria. I focused on arranging my feet correctly, relaxing my throat, and drawing a deep breath.

I glanced at the audience and was startled to see Mother sitting on the back row. I had expected her, but she must have slipped in after I was seated. She looked small, gray, and simple compared to all the glory surrounding her. She was neat and tidy but simply Mother. Nothing more. I felt a twinge of embarrassment at seeing her, so plain and inelegant, so out of place in this crowd of educated, refined society. Yet, as my voice hesitated and struggled to find the opening note, my eyes rested upon her, a safe and familiar spot of security. She smiled, obviously proud of me and wanting my success. At that moment, the rest of the audience disappeared, and I was singing only to her. I forgot to focus on all the things I had studied, thinking instead of the beauty of the music, the joy of the song passing through me, filling me with light and honey-tasting sound.

> But I also dreamt which charmed me most
> that you loved me still the same,
> that you loved me,
> you loved me still the same . . .

My lips closed about the final note, letting it linger upon the air before I finished it precisely as I had been taught. Applause burst from the corners of the room, and I curtseyed low, blushing and beaming.

I returned to my seat, and the programme continued. Madame took my arm and whispered, "Beautifully rendered, Mima. You have truly learned much these months." I beamed again.

I was asked to sing once more before the programme ended. There were several other numbers I enjoyed, once my own performance was past. One man played the violin. He played it elegantly, but I found myself wishing it had a touch more feeling, a pinch more . . . what was it? And I realized I was comparing his playing to Will's, who I now considered to be the ultimate example of violin mastery. I suddenly wished he were there to listen and make some sardonic remark.

After the concert was finished, many of the audience members sought me out to offer congratulations. "I look forward to seeing much more of you, Miss Hough," said Mr. Everton. "I shall expect great things."

I smiled my thanks.

Mother gave me a warm hug. "It was beautiful, Mima. I would not have missed it—you sang divinely," she said. "Your voice has changed," she added thoughtfully.

"Thank you for coming, Mother," I said, but I felt a bit of relief when she left, although the relief was accompanied by guilt. For a seamstress she dressed herself so practically, even when surrounded by glamour.

This glittering world, so elegant and refined, was a place I longed to be, and there stood Mother, so plain and familiar and ordinary. I had come from her, but could I join this new world? Could I be accepted here? In which world did I belong?

Part Three

ST. LOUIS, MISSOURI

1848

CHAPTER THIRTY-FOUR

*T*hree years passed away with sewing and singing. I was happy and full of hope. Madame Leonora continued to teach me. I learned how to sustain notes and properly form words. My lung capacity increased. I sang in concerts and choirs and met the best musicians of the city. There were balls and parties at the Concert Hall, and yes, occasionally even suitors. I began to feel that I belonged in this place. I planted the cabbage roses from Providence House on the balcony in ceramic pots. On warm summer days they climbed the railing and bloomed in clusters of sweet pink blossoms. When breezes carried their fragrance inside, I felt I was home.

But one day Mother said to me, "Brigham Young has settled the

Mormons in the West. They have built a city called Salt Lake in the Rocky Mountains. They're planning to build another temple."

A cold dread settled in the bottom of my stomach, and I looked at her sharply. "Will the Bennions be leaving?"

"I do not know, but many of the Saints here feel it is time to join the rest of the Church. Many will go."

"But some will stay?"

"Perhaps."

"I do not wish to leave this city," I told her. "I wish to stay here. Always."

"I know," said Mother. Her eyes were sad, and I knew she longed to go.

"How could you wish to leave?" I asked. "There are churches everywhere."

"But there is only one Zion," she replied.

"There is no such place," I said.

She turned away, looking suddenly old and tired. I squirmed with guilt, but I knew she would not leave me. I did not think I could survive starting over again.

But Mary Bennion did leave. In the spring, she and Samuel bought supplies to be shipped upriver, where a covered wagon was waiting. When she left, tears traced the contours of her face. I held her close. "Good-bye, dear Mary. Shall we meet again?"

"If it is God's will," she said.

"I wish you would stay," I said simply.

Mary glanced at her husband and then back at me. "It is a lovely city. You have a bright future here. I pray you will be happy. Write to me."

"I will," I promised.

I watched them leave—Samuel, Mary, John, who was eight now, and little Elizabeth, who was five. Mary believed she was carrying another child, and I wondered where this new journey would take them. I could not understand why Samuel would make his family leave their home yet again.

Was it really God who asked them to leave safety for the wilderness? Who was this God who would ask such a thing? As little John waved good-bye, I remembered the broken nest he had found in Nauvoo long ago. I hoped they would find safety.

One day as I sat in Phillips Music Store, Madame Leonora finished helping a customer and turned to me. "Mima, your Mother is a Mormon, yes?"

I nodded.

"I have heard they have some beautiful new hymns."

"Perhaps," I said. "My mother has not mentioned any for quite a while." I did not tell her that was because I had asked Mother to stop showing me Mormon hymns.

"I am told they have some talented composers, and I would like to see some scores. Do you think your mother would be willing to send some?"

"I am certain she would," I sighed. Madame Leonora glanced at me, and I gave her a shallow smile. "I will bring them." I knew Mother would be thrilled to provide me with music, and I could not refuse Madame Leonora, but I had no desire to discuss it with Mother.

At dinner that evening, I tried to mention the subject casually. I cleared my throat. "Madame Leonora is wondering if you could provide the scores for new hymns."

"Hymns from the Mormon services?" she asked. Her voice was eager and surprised.

"I suppose so," I said cheekily.

Her face lit up with a smile, and I felt a touch of guilt.

"Certainly, Mima," she said. "There are many I have longed to share with you, but I thought you would not be interested."

"I am not," I said. "Madame Leonora would like them."

The smile faded from her face. "Very well," she said.

I cringed and wondered if I was the cruelest daughter alive.

A few days later, Mother brought home a wrapped package. "The scores," she said. "For Madame Leonora. Please tell her that the song entitled 'My Father in Heaven' was written by Sister Eliza Snow in Nauvoo. We have been trying to find music to suit it. One option is included, but perhaps Madame Leonora could think of another melody that would be more fitting."

"Thank you," I said meekly, as I took the package.

Madame Leonora opened it at the store the next day. She exclaimed over several pieces. "Lovely," she said. "What talented poets the Mormons have. Pity they are such fanatics, but perhaps it is good for their art."

I told her about Eliza Snow's song. She read the lyrics. "Lovely," she murmured again. "Strange, yet striking. But what tune?" She set down the page and began rifling through a stack of papers.

I took up the paper and read the words:

> *O my Father, thou that dwellest*
> *in the high and glorious place.*
> *When shall I regain thy presence*
> *and again behold thy face?*

Shock ran through me. What was this song? The author was speaking to God as if she knew Him. As if He was someone you could talk to like any other person. It was thrilling, in an appalling sort of way. *But that is not what God is,* I thought. God is everywhere, nowhere, without shape or form. Isn't He?

I helped Madame Leonora search through stacks of papers, looking for a tune to match the words. She finished, exhausted. "I cannot quite seem to place it," she said. "It seems that I know, but I cannot recall. Perhaps it will come to me as I sleep tonight."

But I doubted that it would. In my opinion those words did not deserve to be set to music. They were different from any hymn I had heard before. Were they blasphemy? I was not sure. They made God so common, so familiar, so ungodlike. We looked through several other hymns, and Madame Leonora thanked me for giving her the scores.

When I left the store that day I could hear the Voice of Rector Buckley reciting the Athanasian Creed in my head. "The Father incomprehensible, the Son incomprehensible, and the Holy Ghost incomprehensible." Incomprehensible. Unknowable. That was who God was. Wasn't He?

That night it was I who dreamed. In my dream, I walked with Mary alongside a covered wagon. The sun beat down upon us, and dust from the wagon wheels clung to our noses and mouths. The road wound up a mountain, snaking back and forth, higher and higher into the air. As we climbed, the air grew clearer. Finally we reached a vista. From the top of the mountain, I could see across the prairie to the long line of wagons trailing behind us. Beyond the wagons I thought I could see a glimmer of a shimmering ocean. In the valley below, a man removed his hat from his head and waved, beckoning me. I knew at once that it was Father. I had never seen him so clearly in my life. I could see the sparkle of his hazel eyes, the exact color of my own, and the dimple in his firm chin. I tried hungrily to memorize the shape of his nose, the lines of his strong, capable hands.

He cupped his hands around his mouth and called to me. I could not hear what he was saying. He called again, and still I could not hear. I quieted the horses, hushed the wind, and settled the dust. Then I removed my bonnet, pulled back my hair, and turned towards him, straining with all my might. His voice came again. I understood him this time.

"Come home, Mima," he called. "Come home."

"Where is home?" I called back to him. But the wind picked up my voice, carried it over the cliffs, and dropped it in a ravine. He did not hear me. "Where is home?" I shouted louder. He turned away and walked into the valley. He could not hear me. Perhaps he thought I did not hear him. Perhaps he thought I did not care. I knelt down in the dust and wept. The hot wind dried my tears right on my face; they turned to salt on my cheeks. "Father," I cried. "Come back!"

I awoke and found myself bound by hot, sweaty blankets. I threw off the blankets and lay panting in the darkness. "It was only a dream," I told myself over and over. "It was only a dream."

CHAPTER THIRTY-FIVE

ummer turned to fall. One day as I stood on the balcony, clipping the last of the cabbage roses, Mother stepped out, a thin letter in her hand. "From Mary," she said.

"Thank you," I said, tearing it open. I smoothed the sheet of paper, anxious for news of my friend.

> Dear Mima,
>
> Hope you are well. We have joined a company of Saints going to Salt Lake. We have food, and so far the weather has held. We hope to arrive in Salt Lake in August. The walking is tedious, but the sights are lovely. Wide open skies, fields of flowers, and buffalo. Almost every night we sing, play music, and dance. I

think of you and wish you were here to sing for us. Do
you remember the nights we danced under the stars
on the Parthenon?
  Much love,
  Mary

I sighed with relief to know that my friend was safe. And relatively happy. The memory of dancing on the *Parthenon* made me think of the owner of the violin that was still hidden safely in its case under my bed. Sometimes I imagined receiving a letter from him or meeting him by accident on a street corner. I wondered what I would say. I wondered what I would feel.

"What is Mary's news?" asked Mother.

I handed her the letter and turned back to my roses. She read the letter and watched me among the flowers.

"It sounds lovely, doesn't it?" Mother said. "Fields of flowers and singing under the stars?"

The feeling of dread settled back in my stomach. "Walking across a continent, in search of something that doesn't exist?" I asked. "I don't think it sounds lovely."

Snip. Snip. I cut the flowers viciously and tossed the dead blossoms into the street below.

The following spring, many Germans arrived in St. Louis, bringing with them a strain of cholera that made its way through the city. Whooping cough spread as well, until many people were frightened to leave their homes. The greatest suffering was among the poor immigrants. The Irish and German arrivals died by the score. Madame Leonora closed the music store. "Just until this dreadful plague is past," she promised. "Stay home, Mima. You should not risk your voice."

Mother and her fellow Mormons gave aid to those who were suffering. "Come with me, Mima," she said to me one day. "They are suffering severely. You should see the children. It is awful."

I considered what to do: hide in my apartment or try to help? I remembered the beggars I had seen on the streets in Liverpool, grabbing at the carriage as we passed. I had longed to help them, but I had also feared them. And of course, what if we caught the disease ourselves?

I baked bread and made soup for Mother to take to the sufferers, but I stayed home, practicing songs and hoping the music store would reopen soon. But the plague only grew worse. Soon the church bells rang day and night, mourning the dead. One day when Mother came home, her eyes held despair. "The cemeteries are full," she said. I cringed with horror.

She was right. Soon bodies were piled into open wagons and pulled through the streets. I knew they would be taken outside the city and burned. I no longer wanted to be on the balcony to see the death carts pass by and hear the incessant ringing of the church bells.

No one knew what caused the plague. Rumors flew. Some people claimed it was the immigrants' unusual food. Still Mother continued to help. I begged her to stay home. She refused, yet she did not catch the dreaded illnesses. I wanted to stay in St. Louis and sing. Perhaps if I helped Mother, God would let us stay. Did it work that way?

"I will go with you," I told her at last.

"Thank you, Mima," she said. "We will visit a German family on Wednesday. They suffer terribly."

"But, Mother," I protested, "Madame Leonora says it is the Germans' sauerkraut that is causing the cholera epidemic."

"Such a belief is silly and ignorant, Mima. Surely you must see that."

"But there are so many dead. Just leave the food outside the door. There is no need to risk your own life."

"Did Jesus tell the leper to stay away, fearing for his own health? Of course I'll go in. They need me." I felt her reproach and knew she was right.

"I'll go too," I said. *We can die together,* I thought.

When we left the house, the streets were eerily quiet. We walked several blocks to an immigrant neighborhood.

"Right here." Mother stopped me in front of a dark and miserable shack. Inside its two small rooms lived the immigrant family. The father opened the door, his face pinched and gaunt. On the bed, the mother moaned, and three thin children curled around her for warmth. Mother went to the woman, and the woman's hand reached out to her. There were tears in her eyes and in my mother's. "*Danke,*" the woman whispered. Mother lifted one of the miserable children and spooned broth into its mouth. The child pressed both hands to its stomach.

I watched my mother in awe. How could she hold the filthy thing without cringing? It coughed in her face, and I flinched. I wished I could hide my repulsion. I moved to the fire, added wood from their small supply, sweeping the hearth, searching for something to do away from the bed. The father drew close to me, touching my sleeve. I snatched back my arm as if his touch was hot. "*Danke,*" he said. "*Danke schön.*" Suddenly he coughed.

"You're welcome." I nodded, wiping my cheek. I tried to smile and then bent over the fire to hide my face.

Mother fed the family capsules of opium and pulverized black pepper. When she was sure she had done everything she could, we left. The German mother and two of her children were dead by Friday. On Tuesday my own fever began.

When I awoke, my head was heavy, so heavy I found it difficult to rise from the pillow. Mother took one look at me and took me straight back to bed, where I lay, sometimes in sleep, sometimes awake, mostly hovering somewhere in between. My dreams were filled with ragged children, dark shacks, and licking flames. At times I thought I was back on the ship, my body cold and damp, with an endless rocking that was only in my head.

As she had cradled the German child, Mother laid cool cloths against my head and spooned broth between my lips. I saw her relief that it was not cholera. But after two weeks, when the fever subsided and I began coughing, her brow furrowed with new worry. One day I rose from bed, coughing and gasping, straining for breath. I clawed the air, trying to breathe through the monster that had me by the throat. I felt as if I were drowning. Mother ran to my side and held me through the terror. When it was over, her eyes were full of shadows. "Whooping cough," she whispered as she wrapped me in her arms. "The German father had whooping cough too." My lungs spasmed in coughing fits that seemed endless. I coughed until a piercing pain began in my ribs, a pain that burned with every breath.

In the first days I felt my body fighting back. The fever ravaged me on the outside, but inside I still felt the strength of a healthy body, strong from months of walking and singing. But as the days turned into weeks and another rib cracked from coughing, I felt my strength draining away.

The weeks that followed were gray and shapeless. The winter sun outside my window mocked me. My days consisted of holding onto the time between the suffocating coughing fits. Every breath hurt. All my strength was gone, and I had damaged my throat as well as my ribs. My mind empty of music, I couldn't imagine ever singing again. I was lost in the gray mist of illness, and desire for life passed from me.

My mother saw it go, and this caused her greater fear, more even than the fever had done. "You must fight, Mima," she pleaded. But I did not want to fight. Perhaps if I died she could go to Zion, as she wanted. She could travel on to the white city in the West. And I could rest without the wracking cough that seemed it would break my body in pieces.

That night I turned my head away when Mother brought soup. I would not eat it, even though she begged. She left in tears as I turned my head to the wall and drifted into the gray mist. I dreamt of the sea again, shimmering grays, a thousand colors of gray. Cold, lifeless, surging in a swell. I wanted to slip into those cold, gray waves and float suspended forever. My bones would break apart and become soft and

smooth, like the sea glass. Then suddenly I was back in the Germans'
shack, in front of flames, miserable, wishing to be anywhere else. The
father inched towards me, and I moved closer toward the fire to avoid
him, closer and closer to the flames until I felt the heat searing my
hands, burning into my face, my arms, my skirts. The flames reached
for me.

"Mima." Mother was shaking me awake. "Mima, you must get up.
The city is on fire." I struggled upwards from the dream, forgetting
about my broken ribs until the pain seared through my side. I turned
back to the wall, but Mother lifted me from the bed. "You are coming
with me," she said. She set me on my feet and threw a shawl around
me. I had not strength to fight her. She gathered a satchel and led me
from the room. Out the window I saw a far-off orange glow against the
dark sky.

"Where will we go?" I asked.

"To the roof," she replied. "It is the only place to see which way the
fire is moving."

Up, up, up we climbed.

I had to rest, gasping for breath, coughing, pain splitting my side.
Others climbing with us soon passed us, but Mother wouldn't let me
rest for long. I let her pull me on in spite of the pain that stabbed my
ribs with each step.

At last we were on the roof. We gasped at the sight. The city was
wrapped in flames. There were two fires: one to the south, and one
to the north. Flames burning through the night had consumed whole
buildings, clawing the sky as if they would climb right up to the moon.

The sky was blanketed in smoke, dark even though the sun would soon rise. The stench of burning was horrendous. Every church bell in the city rang out warning, and in the distance, beyond the fires, we saw the river, the cold water mocking as it slipped into darkness.

Mother and I clung to each other in terror. "Oh, Mima," she cried. "The lovely city."

"It's gone," I said. A roof on a distant building collapsed and showers of sparks exploded into the air. The air was filled with horrible black billowing smoke, and I was not the only person coughing. My eyes traced the remains of the skyline, looking for the stately Old Cathedral, so close to Phillips Music Store. "Please, God," I whispered, "save the music store. In case I ever can sing again. Please save the store." It seemed safe for the moment, but the fire was spreading quickly, jumping from rooftop to rooftop. The narrow streets that I had found so charming, so much like home, had become a fire trap now.

"Oh, God," Mother said, her eyes closed in prayer, "please spare this city. Spare these people. In Jesus' name, amen." She opened her eyes. "First cholera and now this. What have we done?"

It was true, I realized. It was like a heavenly condemnation. I thought of Mother's desire to go west. Perhaps God had wanted her to go, and I'd refused to let her. I thought of Jonah, trying to run from God upon the seas. The storm that had chased his ship, nearly consuming it. Cholera and now the fire seemed like heaven-sent plagues, as in the days of Moses. "Let my people go!" the flames seemed to scream.

The flames jumped ever closer to the Old Cathedral and the store.

I gripped Mother's hand, hoping the historic building would not be next. Suddenly there was a fierce explosion of gunpowder not far from the cathedral. The blast clutched and shook the city, as a ball of fire lit the sky and several buildings exploded.

"That was man-made. It must be a fire break," said a man next to me. "They're trying to save the Old Cathedral."

As the fire turned to blackness, we could see that their plan had worked. The Old Cathedral was standing, but the empty space next to it broke my heart. "The music store is gone," I sobbed. Mother held me as I cried. The pianofortes, the violins on the walls, the rows and rows of music books: all that lovely sound blown to pieces in an instant. "There is nothing left in this city for me. Nothing."

I clung to her and said at last, "I will go west with you."

Mother wiped the tears from my face. "No, Mima. We'll stay here."

"There is nothing here to keep us. I will go." And in that dawn as dark as night, wrapped in smoke and flames and the clanging of church bells, I felt, strangely, that I had been brought back to life.

CHAPTER THIRTY-SIX

Although I continued to improve from the day of the fire, my convalescence was maddeningly slow. My ribs healed first, and I could eventually move and bend without sharp pain. My cough lingered for months, however, and frequently I coughed until vomit rose in my throat. Worst of all, I could not sing. My lungs and ribs were fragile; they could not support my breath. My vocal cords were raw and sore, and I could not breathe without coughing. Even leaving my pianoforte was nothing compared to this agony. My head was full of songs, but my mouth could not form them.

The cholera grew worse throughout the summer. The plague had left so many dead that the churches stopped the constant ringing of their bells. People left the city in droves.

Near the end of the summer, Madame Leonora visited me. When she heard my voice, she shook her head. "I am truly sorry, Mima. I know what this means to you. You have great talent. I pray your health will return."

I nodded, my eyes filled with tears. "We are leaving this city," I told her, "to join the Mormons in the Salt Lake Valley."

"Perhaps your lungs will heal on the journey," she said. "We also will leave the city. We are going to New Orleans, where we have family. Perhaps someday there will be another store."

"I am sorry," I said.

"As am I. So many people in the city are suffering; why should we be different? More die of cholera every day. It will take years to rebuild from the fire. It seems there is a curse upon St. Louis."

I thought of Jonah and the day of the fire. "Perhaps the curse will soon be lifted."

"I pray it may be, or there will be no one left to bury the dead."

When she left, I knew that I would never see her again. There was still so much I desired to learn from her, so many things that I wished we could have discussed. But I could not sing. Perhaps I would never sing again.

Before she left she pressed a book into my hands: *The Sacred Harp.* "Do not give up, Mima," she said. "God gave you a talent. He will help you find a way to use it."

A sob caught in my throat. "Thank you," I said, but to me it seemed that God was doing everything possible to keep me from using my gift.

After Madame Leonora left, I pushed the book under my bed, where I would not have to look at it.

During the long months of my winter convalescence, I noticed that Mother spent hours poring over lists. At first I thought they were sewing lists, but soon I realized that she was planning our departure. She was determining costs and supplies we would need. Finally she showed me her figures.

"We will have two wagons," Mother said. "There will be little fabric in Salt Lake, and if we wish to continue to support ourselves, we will need to take much of the store with us. This is a list of food that is recommended we take with us."

I looked over her shoulder. "A thousand pounds of flour, three sheep, a milk cow, a musket and powder, tea, coffee, sugar, pepper, dried beef, dried fruit, etc."

"How do we find all this?" I asked.

"We will give the list of supplies and the money to Brother Peters. He will make arrangements. Then we will travel by steamship upriver to St. Joseph, where our teams will be waiting."

"And who will drive the teams, pray tell?"

"We will, of course."

"You and I?" I asked. "We know nothing of driving oxen."

"Then we will learn."

I tried to imagine Mother and me driving two covered wagons over the dusty road of my dream. The road to the West. Was it the road to Father? I imagined the wagon breaking down, burning up, floating away in a river, and doing anything other than arriving safely.

Two days later Mother came home from a Church meeting. Her cheeks were flushed, and her hands refused to be still—they moved from her hat to her waist to her papers and back to her hat. "I spoke with Brother Peters today," she said. "I told him of our plan. He said it would be better if we had a young man drive one of the wagons. Then you and I could take turns with the other."

"And where are we to find a young man?" I asked with a smirk.

"Brother Peters knows of one who wishes to go West. He has no family with him and would be pleased to assist us."

"Well, then, it seems it is settled," I said, wondering at her excitement. Nothing about the trip seemed settled to me in the least. Actually it was the most unsettling proposition I had ever considered.

"Would you like to know the young man's name?"

"I am sure I will be sick of hearing it eventually, Mother," I said.

"Yes, but as you know it already, you may wish to hear it again. It is Will Farndon."

Oddly, it seemed that my stomach was lying on the floor. Mother chuckled, and I could not do anything to hide my shock.

I saw him first at the St. Louis levee. We would travel by steamship to the outfitting point. The gangplank was placed, and people rushed here and there, carrying cargo onto the boat. People scurried in every direction, but Will was leaning against a crate, staring out at the river, his hands in his pockets. He had grown taller in the years since I had last seen him. And thinner. He felt my gaze upon him, and at last he turned. His eyes were still the color of coffee, and his smile still reached his eyes. He tipped his hat to Mother and me. "Good morning, Sister Hough, Miss Mima."

"Good morning, Mr. Farndon," Mother replied.

"It has been a long time since we last met," he said. "Miss Mima, you've grown taller."

I blushed. "Much has happened since Mary's party," I said.

"Much indeed," he said. Did I detect bitterness in his voice? "I have heard that I will have the pleasure of driving your wagon to the Salt Lake Valley."

"We are grateful," said Mother.

"As am I," said Will.

"All aboard," shouted the captain. We mounted the gangplank, and within an hour St. Louis was slipping into the water, just as Liverpool and Nauvoo had done before. The steamboat's whistle blew, a deep, throaty rumble, beginning low and growing louder. The turning of the great paddle wheel created a rhythmic churning, and black smoke billowed from the smokestacks. I leaned against the railing, bidding goodbye to the Old Cathedral and the hole in the city where the music store had once stood. I bade good-bye to our apartment, which had not been home as Providence House had been but was a place where I had hoped to stay. I bade good-bye to the cholera victims and the German man who gave me whooping cough in exchange for my voice.

I crossed the ship to the front railing. We traveled up the Mississippi River for a short time and then turned west up the Missouri River. We were leaving civilization behind and heading into the wilderness, just as Lewis and Clark had done nearly fifty years before. In the weeks before leaving St. Louis, we had been told many discouraging tales about the dangers of the Missouri River. In addition to the sand-bars, cholera was rampant on the ships, and the lands on either side were wild lands where Indians and strange beasts were said to roam.

But as we slowly moved up the river, I thought that besides being dangerous, it was also lovely. Flat and wide, the water was smooth, albeit muddy. Birds dipped and soared over its surface, and large rocks and cliffs along the bank soared into the sky. The trees were light green with the flush of springtime.

Will stood beside me on the deck and rested his arms on the railing. "I say, this does seem familiar. Could it be we have done this before?"

I laughed. "This steamer is hardly the *Parthenon*."

"Tell me, Miss Mima, do you plan to travel around the whole world by boat?"

"Perhaps," I said. "Although it feels like that was another Mima who left England so long ago."

Will nodded. "It was," he said.

"But traveling helps me think."

"We are standing still, yet moving," he replied.

"Exactly. My mind is free to journey to new places."

"And do you think the water helps?" he asked.

"Thoughts are liquid, flowing into each other, pulling at one like a river current."

"And where does it pull you?"

"To the sea, of course," I said. "'The deep where all our thoughts are drown'd.'"

"To God, then?"

"Perhaps."

"But not all thoughts lead to the ocean. Take this steamer. It is working hard to push against the current."

"Yet it is still being pulled by it."

"But what would happen if it just followed the current?"

"It could stop fighting and go home," I said. I looked at Will. His eyes were dark. What were we discussing? I barely knew. I had never spoken like this with anyone.

"Then perhaps it should stop fighting," he said, his eyes impenetrable.

"Perhaps." I nodded.

"Miss Mima," he said, leaning so close to me that I could smell the scent of his clothes, spicy and pleasant, "before you left Nauvoo, I asked you to keep something for me. I hardly dare to hope that you might still have it. Can you tell me what became of it?"

"We are still settling our things," I said, "but I will have something for you soon." His eyes filled with hope, softly shining, and I could see how much this meant to him.

"Mima," Mother called from across the deck. "Please come and help me with these parcels." I hastily curtseyed and dashed away. I felt his eyes follow me across the deck.

CHAPTER THIRTY-SEVEN

That evening Mother and I went up on deck for the sunset. I caught my breath at the change in the world. The sky was stained with bright pinks and purples. The river was flat and glassy, and the color spilled out of the sky onto the river. It seemed we had floated into a stained glass window. The banks of the river were soft, black secrets, hovering along the edge of the rosy light.

"Mima," said Mother, "have you ever seen anything so ethereal?"

"Is this what heaven looks like, do you suppose?"

"I imagine heaven must look like all the most beautiful places in the world," she said. "This is surely one of them."

"Would Father like this heaven?"

"It is hard for me to imagine your father thinking any place lovely other than the Box," said Mother. "He used to say that he would not trade Providence House to the Queen if she offered him Windsor Castle. But perhaps he has changed his opinion since seeing heaven."

"Do you believe that Father is still Father?" I asked. "Or do you suppose he is mixed up in the clouds and sky and water?" *Please don't be preachy,* I prayed silently.

Mother looked over the pink waters. The black was spilling off the banks and into the water now. "I think perhaps it is both of those, Mima."

"Both?"

"I think he *is* still Father. Still the same person who loved us. Yet I also feel him when I see the clouds and sky and water. Not mixed up with them but a part of them somehow. I do not know how to explain."

"You told Mary that you knew him," I said.

She nodded slowly. "Yes, I still know him, Mima."

I waited for her to say more.

"Not in the way you might think, but I feel him with me at times."

"When?" I asked.

"Sometimes when I'm sad. When I see beauty. When I hear you sing. I feel God at those times, but beside Him I feel your father. It is hard to explain."

My heart ached. "I want to feel him too," I said. But I did not say it aloud. I said it in my mind, and I said it to the pink sky and the clouds. And mostly I said it to the river. I hoped it would carry my wish back to the ocean. Back to God. A piece of glass—sharp, brittle, and cruel.

The next day, I found a spot at the rear of the main deck, directly above the churning wheel. I loved watching the wheel cut into the water, breaking the smooth, glassy surface into white foam. Not many yards behind the wheel, the water returned to smoothness with only a few bubbles left on the surface to show that anything had happened. Yet I felt sure it was causing havoc underneath the surface. The vessel left a swath of dirt and sand swirled through the water, disturbing depths long settled.

I remembered my favorite corner on the *Parthenon,* where I would sing for the ocean. I longed to sing again. I could hear the words and notes in my head. I could hear my voice in my mind so clearly that I was sure I would be able to really sing. But when I opened my mouth and drew a deep breath, my lungs spasmed and I bent double, coughing and coughing.

When I stopped, I leaned over the railing, pure bitterness in my heart. As if to mock me, a river bird flew low overhead, calling out with a shrill cry. The paddle churned the water, and the whistle sounded. Everything in the world could make sound except for me.

Will found me there in a black mood. "Good day, Miss Mima."

"Is it?" I asked.

"Well, the weather is fair, so it can be a good day, if you wish to be on a steamer bound for St. Joseph."

"It doesn't matter where I am bound," I said.

"Do you wish you had stayed in England?"

"Yes. No. That is, I am unsure."

"Come now, where is the pioneering spirit? Just think of all the lands awaiting discovery before us. Perhaps we need a song to raise your spirits, a song of the West. Truly it has been too many years since last I heard you sing."

I turned my face to him, more miserable than ever.

"What is it?"

"I cannot sing. I had whooping cough several months ago. It damaged my lungs, my throat, my ribs—it robbed me of my voice."

His eyebrows drew together. He did not say, "I'm sorry," and I could have hugged him for withholding the pity.

"An odd feeling if your head is full of songs."

I smiled at his understanding.

He leaned against the railing. "What is left of the river if you take away the water?"

My eyes burned. But as I thought of Will's similar sorrow, my heart lightened. "One moment," I said. I darted back to the main deck where our cramped cabin was. I rummaged through my trunk and pulled the battered violin case into the light. I had wanted to return this to Will for so long. I carried it carefully back to the deck where I had left him. He saw me coming, saw what I carried. He stepped toward me, a look of longing on his face. I placed it into his hands. He sat down and bent his head over the case. Then slowly he opened it.

I felt honored to return it to him, as if I was giving him something sacred, like returning a child to its mother. I thought of Mary seeing John again when she thought she had lost him. I imagined someone handing me back my voice.

Will lifted out the violin, so elegant in shape. He touched it as if he had never seen it before, running his hands over the back and across the neck, lightly touching the strings, one by one.

Just when I thought he had forgotten me completely, he lifted his face to mine. "Mima, I would say that you have no idea what you've returned to me, but I know you do. If I could give you your voice wrapped up in a box, I would. And it reminds me of someone very dear. Thank you."

I nodded. Who had he left behind?

Could I ever forget Will's face when I handed him that violin box? What an odd sensation to lose something so beloved and have it returned again, when you have pictured it over and over in your mind. And then to hold it again, see aspects of it you've forgotten, the curve of the spine, the scratch in the body, the silken finish of the wood. Like going home to Providence House again. Or someone bringing me Father.

Will was tuning the strings now. They needed it badly, of course. When he finished, he strummed them all across. They sounded rich and full and perfect, each resonating with the others, a perfect complement of sound. "Long ago you refused to sing 'Hurrah for California.' Perhaps now you'll reconsider?"

I shook my head.

"Stubborn as well as fair," he said. His eyes gleamed. "Well, then, what about an American tune?" He sounded the first few bars of "Turkey in the Straw." He played several lines and then paused. "Come, Miss Mima. This really isn't the same at all without your voice. Perhaps you will sing what you can?"

"Truly, Mr. Farndon, you will regret asking me if I should try."

"But your voice will never recover if you do *not* try. Come, you have given me back my instrument. Now you sing a bit."

"Do you remember 'The Water Is Wide'?"

"Of course."

He played the opening bars.

"'The water is . . .'"

My lungs spasmed, and I coughed. He stopped playing and waited.

"You see?" I said.

"Try again," he said.

I tried again, with the same result.

"Again," he said.

Every attempt ended in coughing. My stomach began to heave.

"How do you feel?" he asked.

"Like a violin that has been stepped on," I said.

"We will do this every day," he said.

"I'll be sure not to eat beforehand."

His laughter echoed across the deck. I imagined the paddle wheel picking up the sound and smashing it into the river. Down, down, into those dark, undisturbed depths.

As we traveled farther up the Missouri River, mammoth rock cliffs began to rear themselves along the river's edge. Sheer rock faces soared into the sky. Some passengers were afraid of the rocks and stayed below deck, fearing the rocks would tumble into the river. Others felt smothered and confined.

I found them exhilarating, as if this area of earth had tried to heave itself to heaven, a sort of tower of Babel built without hands. I called them mountains, but Mother corrected me.

"We will see true mountains before this journey has come to a close. The Rocky Mountains over which we will pass will be far higher and more treacherous."

I shivered, eyeing the fracture lines in the rocks where basalt and limestone seemed to have been neatly folded like a quilt. In some places huge pieces of rock had sheared off the cliff face and lay scattered beneath them like whitened giant bones.

Will stood beside me, regarding the stones that had fallen. "The rain is turning them back into sand, and then the sand will become rock. Over and over again."

"Do you remember the sea glass Captain Woodbury had on the *Parthenon*?" I asked.

Will nodded. "I saw it a few times. Turquoise shot through with silver."

"Don't you find it remarkable that a piece of something broken and sharp can turn into something smooth and lovely?"

He nodded.

"I like to think that if you have a sorrow and you throw it into the water . . ." I did not look at him. Instead I looked into the water and rushed on. "The ocean will swallow it up and send it back to you rounded and soft."

"But sea glass goes through an awful lot of pounding before it is transformed," Will pointed out. "Immense pounding and lots of time.

And probably some pieces never change. They are simply smashed into a million bits."

"But some become beautiful."

"Yes, some do."

We were silent for several minutes.

Finally Will spoke. "My father went home." His dark eyes scanned the waters. "To England."

"I heard that," I said. "Why did he go?"

"I don't know. He was disgusted by the mobs in Nauvoo. He said he wouldn't bring my mother to such a place."

"And he left you? In St. Louis?" Will nodded. I couldn't believe what I was hearing. "Why didn't you go with him?"

"Because my mother and six brothers and sisters are waiting to come. My passage home would mean that one of them would not be able to come back."

"You stayed in St. Louis alone?" I was amazed. Again, he nodded. "How did you support yourself?"

"I became apprenticed to a painter and took a room with a Mormon family in the city."

"You could have gone home and stayed there."

My sentence was not a comment. It was a question.

He looked away from the water and into my eyes. His face was serious. "I believe we are going to Zion, Mima. My father believes it too. In time he will join us there."

I was silent. I could not imagine Will all alone in an unknown city. I could not imagine a father who would abandon his son.

"But I was not truly alone in St. Louis," he said.

"You weren't?"

"No. In some ways I never felt less alone."

"Who was with you?"

"Music, for one. Although I did not have my violin, I borrowed one from another Mormon in the city. And I have another Father."

I raised my eyebrows and looked at him with a questioning gaze. I really liked Will. I hoped he was not crazy.

He took a deep breath. "Did you know that according to Mormon belief, God is literally our Father? Not just metaphorically?"

I remembered the song by Eliza Snow. I nodded. "But how could that be possible?"

"He is the Father of our spirit, and we lived with Him before this earth."

I looked at him incredulously.

"The Bible says we are created in His image. So don't you think it would make sense if He looked like us?"

"No," I said.

"Why not?"

"I don't know . . ." I said. "Because He is everywhere and nowhere."

"But He hears our words and speaks to us."

"He speaks to *us?*"

"Well, if He is our Father, don't you think He would speak to us?" Will asked.

"But that is so ungodlike."

"Why?"

"Because God made everything," I said. "He knows everything and is everywhere. He is mighty and all-powerful and omniscient. A human father is close and intimate and . . . real."

"Why couldn't He be both of those things?"

I shook my head.

Know all the stars *and* know me? Speak to prophets *and* to me? Be everywhere *and* right beside me on this boat? I knew that God knew of me because He knew everything. But thinking of Him as a literal Father was entirely different. Could I believe it? Did I dare believe it?

Will watched the struggle on my face and smiled. "I remember when I first was presented with the idea by the missionaries in England. It's a bit of a shock compared to all that you have learned about God. Disturbing yet exciting, perhaps?"

I studied the water, hardly sure of what I felt, and then glanced into his deep, kind eyes and nodded.

CHAPTER THIRTY-EIGHT

 $\mathcal{M}$ other and I finished supper one evening when we were drawing close to St. Joseph. As we walked back to our cabin, we heard the strains of Will's violin.

"Shall we walk up on deck?" Mother asked.

"Yes," I said.

We walked in the direction of the sound. The spring night was chilly but clear. The only lights were from the steamer. The land was a black shadow that slipped away beyond the waters. The stars were spilled out like salt across the sky—full and rich and luminous, so bright I felt I could reach and scoop up a handful.

The rise and fall of the violin was haunting. Will was play-ing Mozart. The melody soared and dived, throaty, full of longing. I wondered who he thought of while he played. The girl he left behind? His father? What if he was thinking of me? The thought made me walk a little faster.

Moonlight fell over him like a charm. Mother and I hesitated. He looked up.

"Miss Mima, Sister Hough, please join me."

"We don't wish to disturb you."

"You are not disturbing me," he said. "Sister Hough, have you heard Mima's exercises? She is making excellent progress."

"Ridiculous. I'm doing nothing of the sort," I said.

"Yes, you are, but we have not practiced yet today. Let your mother hear."

"Very well, but I hardly think she will recognize it as progress."

Will played the opening measures. I began. *The water is wide, I cannot cross o'er.*

As they always did, my lungs contracted, and I turned away to cough.

"There. You see?" said Will, as pleased as if I had just performed an aria.

Mother's eyes were full of pity. "It will come, Mima."

"It has been many months," I said.

"It will come," Mother repeated.

I turned to Will. "What have you been playing under the moonlight?"

"A little Mozart, a few hymns. Have you heard the new hymn by Sister Snow?"

"I've only seen the poem," I said.

"I must play it for you," he said. "Sister Hough, will you sing the words?"

"I've hardly Mima's talent for singing," she said.

"Mima can sing it herself in a few more months."

Will began the opening bars. The melody was vaguely familiar. I was sure I'd heard it somewhere before. But when Mother began to sing, all I heard were the words.

> *O my Father, thou that dwellest*
> *in the high and glorious place.*
> *When shall I regain thy presence*
> *and again behold thy face?*

As they had the first time I heard them, the audacity of the words and their familiarity with the divine took my breath away. The author was speaking to God as if she expected an answer.

It seemed less shocking than before but just as blasphemous.

When he finished the song, Will said, "Music and water seem to go together."

I walked to the railing and looked out at the river, gleaming like a dark satin ribbon. "Music is like water," I said, drawing close to him.

"How so?"

"The melody is like the surface of the water, easily seen. The notes and rhythm are like the hidden currents, the sandbars, and the murky depths below. But the whole thing pulls you forward in one direction, leading you on a journey."

"To the ocean," said Will.

"Yes, to the ocean."

"I like that thought," said Will. "When I'm upon dry land, I'll remember that I can travel down a river whenever I like."

"Without having to eat stale bread," I said.

Will laughed. Impulsively, he leaned forward and brushed his hand along my chin so quickly I wondered afterwards if I had imagined it. But I knew that I had not, for my skin burned with heat where his hand had rested. He dropped his eyes to the water, and the moment, too, slipped into the river.

CHAPTER THIRTY-NINE

$\mathcal{W}$e arrived at Belmont Landing, St. Joseph, Missouri, at midday. Once again Mother and I stepped to a ship's balcony to see what awaited us. *How many more times will we do this?* I wondered.

"Have mercy," whispered Mother when the town came into view.

It was nothing but a scrawny frontier town. Sheltered by a bluff, the town was a ragged assortment of scruffy frame houses and muddy streets bustling with gambling houses and houses of ill-repute. The throngs of people were an odd combination of Mormons headed for their Zion and gold-seekers yearning for California. It was not difficult to tell them apart. But even though they looked very different and acted very differently, they both wanted the same thing: to go west. And that meant that they were all haggling for supplies in St. Joseph.

Around the river and up into the hills, the town was a sea of white tents, covered wagons, and oxen pawing the ground. Shopkeepers tried to sell sick mules and skinny cows for three times their worth. Mother hurried us past the gaming halls and saloons as quickly as possible, and suddenly I was twice as glad we had brought Will along.

The leader of our group had our trunks taken to a hotel where we would stay for three nights. Then he took us to see the wagons that had been purchased for us. Seeing the rough hickory wood and canvas covers that made such a fragile roof, I realized that this wooden box would be our home for the next three months. Mother looked as stunned as I felt.

"How will we ever fit everything into two wagons?" said Mother.

"I didn't bring much," said Will. "As long as I can stow my violin and a few clothes, you can fill up the rest."

"Perhaps you should have offered to assist a father and son instead," I said, throwing him a saucy glance.

"Are you saying I may need to carry the violin as well, Miss Mima?" Will asked.

"You haven't seen Mother's fabric collection," I said. "But if it comes down to fabric or Will's violin, I vote for the violin."

Mother's smile was rueful.

We were introduced to Brother Johnson, an American in charge of assisting the Mormons to arrange their supplies. The next morning he led us to a corral where the oxen were kept and pointed out the eight that would be ours. The beasts were large but seemed calm enough. I eyed their horns.

A young man slowly drove his wagon past us. Brother Johnson called out to him. "Ho there! Brother Conrad!"

The young man stopped the wagon and raised a hand in greeting. "Brother Johnson. Good day."

"How about giving a lesson to the newcomers?" Brother Johnson asked.

"Certainly," Brother Conrad answered.

"This is a fine bit of luck," said Brother Johnson, motioning for us to follow him. "You will get a taste of trail life. Not that you will be riding in the wagon much, hopefully." His laugh made me nervous.

Will assisted Mother as she climbed up on the wagon. I did not need his assistance, but I let my hand rest upon his anyway.

The bed of the wagon was loaded with crates, which we used as chairs. Once settled, Brother Conrad called out, "Git up," and the oxen began to plod. Very slowly at first and then only slightly faster.

"We will never arrive in Salt Lake at this pace," I whispered.

Will nodded.

The wagon was certainly not a carriage. As it rolled over the uneven ground, we felt every bump and crest upon the road. I resolved to wear extra petticoats if I rode in the wagon again.

"Whoa!" called our driver. "Would one of you like to try?"

"I would," I said, darting up to the driver's bench. I wanted to get out of the jolting wagon.

Brother Conrad looked surprised. "I thought the young man there would be driving your wagon."

I blushed. Did he think Will and I were married? "Mr. Farndon will drive one wagon," I said. "My mother and I will take turns with the other."

"Beg your pardon," he said.

I climbed out of the wagon without looking in Will's direction and joined Brother Conrad on the ground beside the oxen.

"Now, miss, this here is Rose, and yonder is Daisy. Stand on their left and hold the Moses stick in case they decide to take off. 'Git up' gets 'em started, then it's 'gee' to go right and 'haw' to go left. 'Whoa' to stop."

Standing next to the oxen, I could see that the beasts were much larger than they had seemed before. I looked at one huge hoof. What if they stepped on my foot as they walked? I took the Moses stick, wondering what I could possibly do with the slim stick that would be helpful.

I turned to the oxen and tried to use a stern voice. "Get up!"

They didn't move, and Brother Conrad laughed. "They don't speak the Queen's English, miss."

"Perhaps we should have requested British oxen," I replied. I tried to imitate Brother Conrad's atrocious accent. "Gidyap," I said. Daisy's foot twitched slightly.

"You've gotta say it like you mean it, miss," said Conrad.

I cleared my throat. "Gidyap!" Daisy and Rose must have heard something familiar in what I said because they rambled off. I darted after them, although they were so slow it was not difficult to catch up. The ground sloped gently to the right, so I needed to bring them back around.

Haw or *gee?* What appalling words. Couldn't we teach our own oxen words I might actually want to shout from here to Salt Lake? "Gee!" I called. "Gee!" The oxen rambled to the right, straight down the slope. "Stop!" I shouted, running after them. I heard Mother and Will exclaim as the ride suddenly became exciting.

Brother Conrad ran up to the oxen with a firm hand. "Whoa, there," he said. The beasts ambled to a stop, and I sighed, defeated. "Don't worry," he said, with a grin. "You'll get the hang of it. I've seen worse first attempts."

I could see he loved being the expert of the situation. "Thank you, sir, for risking your team for my lesson."

Mother and Will struggled out of the wagon and joined us. They were both laughing. "For a moment, I thought you were going to dispose of us both and return to England, Miss Mima," said Will.

"I absolutely considered it."

We were still laughing when we returned to the hotel in St. Joseph, a dirty, shabby establishment that failed miserably to look inviting.

We entered the foyer, and a hotel clerk approached us. "A letter has arrived for you, miss."

"A letter?"

I was surprised. He took a letter from the desk and carried it toward me. As he handed the thin folded sheet of paper to me, a sudden cool breeze blew through the door behind us. Mother shivered. The letter trembled in my grasp.

"From Mary," I said, when I saw the fair, straight hand. I broke the seal and unfolded the paper.

Dearest Mima,

I gave birth to a son two months ago. Last week he died. There was no one in this city to baptize the babe before he went.

"No!" I said.

Mother and Will turned towards me, startled.

"No, no, no!" I exclaimed.

"What is it?" Will asked.

But I could not face him. I could not face anyone. I turned to the door and ran back to the street. Searching frantically up and down for any place to be alone, I rushed back to the place where I had driven the oxen. A small copse of trees offered shelter next to a small pond. I fell to the soft earth and lay down like a forest animal. My breath came raw and ragged, and I clutched the earth with my hands. I waited for the sobs to come, but they did not. My breath burned inside my throat. And when I tried to breathe deeply, I coughed and coughed, until I felt I was drowning. When my breathing slowed, I picked up the letter again. It was streaked with dirt.

I continued where I had left off.

Samuel says he is with God because babies do not need baptism, but I wish it had been done all the same.

I can scarcely stand to look at John and Elizabeth. I think only of him. His hands were tiny and perfect.

My arms ache for him. Even when I hold my other
children, they feel empty. Samuel says we will see him
again, but if that is true, I wish I could join him now.
I long to see you. Hurry to Zion.

   Love,

   Mary

I held the letter for a long time, looking at the surface of the pond. It was tranquil and smooth, but I wondered what lay beneath the surface—rotting trees, decaying animals, rocks covered with slime. The water simply reflected the sky. Blue sky, scattered clouds. I looked heavenward and thought about Will's words about God. Could I really talk to Him? Would He really answer me? I had so many questions burning in my chest.

"Are You really there?" I demanded of the sky. "Do You really know me?" I did not hear a response.

In time, darker clouds moved in, and a light, spring rain began to fall. I knew I should go back, that I should not sit in the rain, getting wet and chilled, but the water from the sky suddenly released my unspoken grief, and at last I could cry. Soft and light at first, like the rain, but after a time my tears came in great, gulping sobs. Sobs for Mary losing her child, sobs for Will losing his father. Why did it seem the world was full of loss—the loss of everything important and dearest—while things like shoes and butter dishes and yards of fabric followed you safely around the world? I sobbed until I had no tears left to cry.

I was grateful for the rain because it seemed to keep me company in grief.

After a time, the rain stopped, and the clouds parted. Sun streamed into the meadow. A robin flew past and stopped several yards from me. She pecked at straw and twigs, gathering them in her beak. She paused, looked at me, and then flew off.

Was she building a nest?

"It's no use," I wanted to tell her. "The nest will fall in a storm." Yet I knew she would build it anyway.

It was a strange and stubborn hope the bird had for its chick and Mary had for her baby and Mother had for me, even when I was unkind to her. Maybe especially then. I felt true remorse for the times I had not cared about what she wanted, thinking only of myself.

If God is really my Father, then does He have this hope for me?

A warm comfort began in my heart, spreading outward, until I felt as if a soft quilt had been wrapped around my shoulders. I gasped at how tangible it felt. Peaceful and calm, like the smooth, still surface of the pond now that the rain had stopped. *Yes, God does hope for me,* I thought. And suddenly I knew it was true. I did not think it. I *knew* it. I hugged my arms together, trying to hold onto the feeling. It was still here with me, and I struggled to think what it reminded me of. Providence House. Mother. It felt just like home.

I turned my face to the sun. "Thank You," I said. And I knew that my Fathers heard me. Somehow, in the midst of all the people and mountains and deserts and oceans spread across this wide planet, they both heard me. I felt their hearing right next to their hope.

I stood up. I needed to find Mother and Will. But I would come back to this place—here, or some place like it. I had so many things I still wanted to learn. And whatever I had felt, I wanted to feel it again.

They were waiting for me. Full of worry and fear and love.

"Mima," said Mother, gathering me in her arms.

"I'm sorry," I said, kissing her cheek. "I needed to be alone." I handed her the letter.

She read it, her eyes full of grieving for our friend, and then handed it to Will, who chastised me. "I was about to set off with oxen to find you, Miss Mima."

"Perhaps I should leave again," I said. "I would like to see you try to chase me with oxen."

He laughed. "Anytime."

My cheeks flamed. I wondered if they could see it on my face. How different I felt. Surely they could see. My words, my voice—they were all different somehow. All new.

Will grew serious after reading the letter, though. "The death of a child is different from the death of an adult," he said. "An adult has had a chance to try out living. But a child is all possibility. When a child dies, all of that possibility goes too."

Something about the way he said it, the pain in his eyes, I knew that he was not talking about Mary's child alone.

After I changed into dry clothes, we ate supper and then sat beside the hotel's fireplace. Will brought out his violin. He played a song, haunting and passionate, the liquid sound of mourning. The music said so many things that none of us could say. Inexpressible joy and sorrow all mixed together and poured into sound. The sound a heart makes as it lives and dies and grieves and dares to hope again. He turned it all into music, and I knew that God and Father and Mary's baby in heaven must have heard the sound and listened along with us.

He played "The Water Is Wide," and Mother sang because I could not:

> *The water is wide, I cannot cross o'er*
> *And neither have I wings to fly*
> *Build me a boat that can carry two,*
> *And both shall row, my child and I.*

I had not realized she knew all the words. I held her hand as she sang, grateful to have her beside me.

As the night became deep, the fire burned low, the flames became a mellowed orange, the center glowing hot and white. Mother excused herself to go to bed, glancing at Will as if to decide whether to trust us alone. "Come soon," she said to me. I nodded.

At last Will put down his violin and ran his hands over it, as he had done the day I first returned it to him. He touched the strings, ran his hands gently along the elegant arch of the neck. "My little sister died a few months before Papa and I set sail."

I sought his eyes, but he stared into the flames, mesmerized.

"She was three. The most joyous child. Her laughter was the sweetest part of home. She would run and sit on my lap and say, 'Play for me, Will.' I would play for her, and she would dance. Music was in her soul. And then she got the typhoid. She suffered for a time and then . . . she was dead."

He looked at me now. His eyes were full of pain, and I knew he could nearly see her when he spoke.

"It seemed like she took all music with her. I could not play after she died." He paused. "Until I met you."

"So the person you longed for on the boat," I said. "It was your sister?"

He nodded, and I couldn't help smiling inside. I knew he was reliving heart-wrenching grief, and yet even in the face of death it is impossible to feel only sorrow. There is too much joy mixed up in it all. And I felt joy now.

"I thought you left another," I said.

He looked at me softly and took my hand. "No," he said.

I wanted then to tell him what had happened to me in the field, what I had felt. But it was still too recent, too fresh. I did not know what words to use. And I did not want to desecrate it by speaking aloud.

So I let Will hold my hand and speak of his sister while I stared into the flames and wondered if the source of the heat I felt was the fire, or Will's hand, or the peace of my own heart.

CHAPTER FORTY

*B*ut the next day, I began to wonder about what I had experienced. Had it really happened? Had I just imagined it? I did not want it to slip away, so I decided to tell Will, to say it aloud to make it real.

I found him by the corral, looking at the oxen. He smiled as I approached and gestured to the beasts. "Do you think they will really be able to carry us over the mountains?"

"Why do you think we brought you along?" I asked.

He chuckled. "I'm afraid you may be sorely disappointed," he said. "I don't believe I could pull a wagon. Although I could play you a nice song while you waited for things to improve."

"That will have to do for now, I suppose," I said. I wondered how to tell him what I wanted to say.

He noticed the look on my face. "What is it?" he asked.

"Will, this sounds strange, but I . . . I think I heard God yesterday." I looked at him, hoping he would not call me crazy. "Just like you said that I could. It was so powerful, so strong. I can still feel the taste of it."

"It lingers for a while," said Will. "Sometimes you can't forget."

"I wouldn't want to," I said.

A knowing smile played around his lips.

"But if that is true . . ." I hesitated, struggling for words. "Then does that mean everything I've always believed about God should . . . change?"

"Perhaps," he said.

I felt slightly dizzy and recalled the tilting headstones in the grave-yard at St. Margaret's so long ago when the ground had shifted beneath them.

Will looked at me with those impenetrable, deep eyes. Deep like the river. Deep like music. Deep enough to swim in forever and never find the bottom.

"But I have always told Mother she was crazy. I have always re-sented the Mormons for taking her. If . . ."

"Your mother has found her path," said Will. "You are just begin-ning to discover yours."

I nodded, thinking of Mother's surety when she stepped into the frozen brook. Someday I wanted to be as confident about my own be-lief as she had been that day. I looked at Will and was grateful for the complete acceptance I saw on his face.

"Plus, I rather enjoy playing the role of heretic," I admitted with a coy smile.

"May I kiss you?" Will asked.

"I am not committing to anything," I said, holding up my hand.

"I'll take my chances," he said.

And then he kissed me. A light, soft brush of his lips across mine that set my heart racing like a prairie fire.

I turned to the west. Together we would dance under the stars and wear ourselves out climbing mountains. But I also knew we would have music. Music and the pounding of waters falling again and again, smoothing our pain until it glowed in the sun. And became beautiful.

A NOTE TO THE READER

Historical fiction is a rather strange amalgamation of truth and imagination. Ideally, a book of this genre should be true in a historical sense even as it strives to be true in a metaphoric sense. That is, in retelling stories that are important to a culture, fiction gives us the opportunity to express truth about the human psyche and experience that literal facts alone cannot convey.

I first heard the story of my great-great-great-grandmother Jemima Rushby Hough Midgley from my own grandmother Alice Allred when I was a young girl. I loved listening to my grandmother's stories of our pioneer ancestors and I was particularly drawn to the stories set in England, a place I romanticized and daydreamed about. Reenacting the stories with my grandmother's dress-ups, I often felt that I had been born in the wrong century and would have preferred to grow up with parasols and petticoats.

While a student at Brigham Young University, I had the opportunity to study in England for a semester, during which each student spent a few weeks living with a local family. The list of available choices included a Midgley family living in Yorkshire. I recognized the family name and, knowing that my family was also from Yorkshire, I leapt at the chance to stay with them.

It turned out that I was, in fact, distantly related to this family of Midgleys, and they graciously took me to visit the parish church in Almondbury, where Joshua Midgley (upon whom the character of Will Farndon is based) was born and raised. As I walked through the ancient gravestones, tilted and scoured by time, I glimpsed a piece of my ancestors' lives and was captivated by the thought of trying to piece together their experiences.

I read through the names in the parish records and realized that generations upon generations had been born, raised, and married in the small town, buried and blessed in the Church of England. I imagined the Mormon missionaries coming to the community and the shock their preaching must have caused, along with the inevitable sacrifices and changes my ancestors chose to make to follow a new and strange religion.

These imaginations began working themselves into the story that became this novel. During the process, my research turned up in a variety of sources, many of the pioneer stories that have been incorporated here. The story of the providential lightning flash aboard the ship comes from an account of the ocean crossing of Joshua Midgley.

The characters of Mary Bennion and her husband are based on

real pioneers of the same names, and the births and deaths of their children are recounted accurately. I was intrigued by Mary's story because her husband joined the Church, but she was not baptized until they reached the Salt Lake Valley several years later. I thought about what her conversion process may have been like. Although in reality my ancestor Jemima joined the Church with her mother (also named Jemima), at some point she must have grappled with the questions of the new religion herself. It is the slow development of faith strong enough to rely on during such trials as the ones the pioneers faced that fascinates me.

Although time has been compressed, I have been largely accurate with the steps of the journey of Jemima and her mother from Wooden Box to Liverpool to New Orleans to Nauvoo to St. Louis (where they did, indeed, survive the cholera epidemic and the fire of 1849), and finally to the West. Mima truly loved to sing, and she used her talent in a multitude of ways; Joshua played both the violin and the cello beautifully. It makes me smile to imagine the music they made together under the stars as they walked the long and arduous trail to the Salt Lake Valley.

In the process of researching, I connected with a distant relative of Jemima's, a descendant of her father and his first wife. As I describe in the story, there was actually a great deal of animosity between the family of the first wife and Mima's mother. Through correspondence, I found that the version of the family history my distant relative grew up with is very different from the one I was raised with. This experience reconfirmed that each family tells their own version of stories, emphasizing their own lessons and sources of truth.

Now, many generations later, I do not wish to dispute facts and dates or motives; rather, I feel it is important to recognize that these early converts to the Church and their families were largely neither angels nor demons—they were complex, multifaceted people (not unlike the members of the Church today), who were caught up in a story they little dreamed would later become the pages of history. I am grateful that recently more and more historians, Latter-day Saint and otherwise, have attempted to write about this unique era of history honestly, neither whitewashing nor disparaging. I have tried to build upon their work by writing accurately and with the sensitivity that the subject matter, because it is sacred to many, deserves.

FOR FURTHER READING

Bushman, Richard L. *Joseph Smith, Rough Stone Rolling.* New York: Knopf, 2005.

Erickson, Charlotte. *Leaving England: Essays on British Emigration in the Nineteenth Century.* Ithaca and London: Cornell University Press, 1994.

Hallwas, John E., and Roger D. Launius. *Cultures in Conflict: A Documentary History of the Mormon War in Illinois.* Logan, Utah: Utah State University Press, 1995.

Haven, Charlotte. "A Girl's Letters from Nauvoo." *The Overland Monthly* (San Francisco), December 1890.

Journal of Jane Rio Griffiths Baker. Church History Library and Archives, The Church of Jesus Christ of Latter-day Saints, Salt Lake City.

Ketchum, Liza. *Into a New Country: Eight Remarkable Women of the West.* Boston: Little, Brown, 2000.

Leonard, Glen M. *Nauvoo: A Place of Peace, a People of Promise.* Salt Lake City: Deseret Book; Provo, Utah: Brigham Young University Press, 2002.

Midgley, Kenneth Eardley. *The Midgleys: Utah Pioneers.* Kansas City, Mo.: Lowell Press, 1981.

Sonne, Conway B. *Saints on the Seas: A Maritime History of Mormon Migration.* Salt Lake City: University of Utah Press, 1995.

Warsaw Signal (Warsaw, Illinois), September 3, 1845.

ABOUT THE AUTHOR

Marianne Monson has always adored antique shops, steamer trunks, and old British novels. She attended high school in Naperville, Illinois. She majored in English literature at Brigham Young University, where she particularly enjoyed studying the Brontës, and spent a semester in London. She holds a master of fine arts degree (MFA) in creative writing from Vermont College and enjoys writing books for all ages. She teaches English and creative writing at Portland Community College and loves reading to her children, Nathan and Aria. An active member of The Church of Jesus Christ of Latter-day Saints, Marianne is the Gospel Doctrine teacher in her ward in Hillsboro, Oregon. You can visit her at www.mariannemonson.com or find her on Facebook.